A Mustard Seed Of Faith

Madelene Yahya

Chapbook Press

Schuler Books
2660 28th Street SE
Grand Rapids, MI 49512
(616) 942-7330
www.schulerbooks.com

A Mustard Seed of Faith

ISBN 13: 978195769

Library of Congress Control Number: 2023

Printed in the United States by Chapbook Press.

This Book is fiction. The stories in this book are based on a true story. I want to relate to everyone about faith, which is God's master Plan, and how one decision could have changed the outcome of me not being here. Everything happens for a reason. People are placed in your Life for a reason. God knew before I was born the outcome. To my grandfather, McKinley Newton Sr: I am just a small part of your legacy and I want to thank you God and you –

Madelene (O'Neal) Yahya

Chapter 1

The year was 1905. Theodore Roosevelt was President and he was in the last term of his Presidency. Alcorn University, one of the first Black Public Historically Great Universities, founded in Lorman Mississippi in 1871, started its first semester for the new school year. Lula Hood, a freshman, was making her way to her classes trying to meet new people, as she was in new surroundings. Yes, her Schooling was paid for. Lula was from Alabama, where she had other siblings. She had three brothers who lived back in Alabama. They were really proud of their little sister as she had been the first family member to go to college. Lula had also gotten a job in the kitchen setting tables and washing the dishes.

One busy day with the hustle and bustle of everyday activities, Lula was running trying to get to work after her long day of classes.   She bumped into this man when she wasn't looking. Her books fell from her hands to the floor.   This man said to Lula, "I'm so sorry."   Then being a little upset and a little embarrassed, Lula started picking her things up off of the floor.   The very nice man also helped Her pick her books up.   When he handed her things to her, he held her hand and their eyes locked in for a very intense contact. The man said to her, "hi my name is Henry, Henry Nixon. "   He also had the biggest smile on his face.   Henry asked her, "What is your name?"   She answered real low, Lula, Lula Hood.   Henry said, very nice to meet you.   Lula smiled and said "likewise" with her books purse in her arms.   As they both had parted, walking in opposite directions, they kept looking back at each other.   Lula made her way to the dining room. At the college, getting through the work shift, she could only think about doing her homework.   Missing one of her classes, vowing to make sure she wouldn't miss going to class, Lula wanted to do her best.   She wanted to get a good night's sleep.

In the morning, Lula was getting ready for class, getting dressed in a long skirt with a shirt that came to her elbow, thick stockings and flat brown shoes all laced up at the front. All dressed, walking to her class, she found herself an empty seat.   Once entering the inside of the room, all of the seats were taken; she was forced to sit in one of the desks that was closest to the professor's desk.   This was an English class. Lula was sitting with her head in her book, looking down.   The professor walked in.   Lula was still looking down; a little scared about being behind.   The professor was taking roll call and also starting to say "Good morning. My name is Henry Nixon."   Lula's head jumps up and then her eyes locked to the professor. Never not being unprofessional teaching his class as he had told Lula, she was a little surprised thinking I know he knows me from the other day. When class was over Professor Nixon said to Ms. Hood, "can I have a word with you?" Lula walks back and said "yes professor." Now as you may or may not know, you have already missed one day of class. I just wanted you to know after missing 3 days of classes without having an extreme emergency; I will have to fail you. Lula looking at him, not being sure of his strong tone was wondering (puzzled) thinking about how he was looking at her the other day. Wow! Did I read him wrong? Lula made her way to her next class. This went on until the end of the semester, which ended in December. She made sure that she had gotten her lessons, staying focused on her classes. The last day of class arrived and she took her exam. She waited very patiently to find out her final grade for the semester. Professor Nixon had called everyone up for their grade. Lula was getting very nervous. She was the last person in the room. He said, "You have gotten an "A" for your grade." He handed her paper with the information on it and said, "job well done." Lula said, "thank you." As she turned to leave the room, Professor Henry grabbed her hand. Then as he was holding her hand, with his other hand, he brushed the side of her face, leaned over, and kissed her. Lula pulled away and said, "What are you doing?" Professor Henry said, "You don't feel it?" Lula said, "What?" The Professor then pulled her closer to him, grabbing her around her waist. Lula didn't stop him this time.   She felt the butterflies in her stomach as Professor Henry kissed her long and very

passionate. Her body very close to the professor, she could feel his
body.   The professor did not know that Lula had never ever been
kissed.   Yes, she was a virgin.   Lula was all into the kiss.
Feeling her under wear getting wet and the professor groin get real
hard, she wanted to know more, but pulled away from him saying,
"NO! Professor Henry said, "Ok."   Lula asked him, "What are you
doing?"   The professor said, "We are just feeling what is real. the
here and now."   Lula said, "I have to go. I have to go to work."
The professor said, "Okay, can I see you another time?"   Lula
said, "Yes, I would like that."   He grabbed her hand with both
hands and then kissed them.   Lula walked away out of the door
with a big smile on her face.   She was thinking, WOW! What is
this feeling? She said to herself, "I have to stay focused. "She put
herself back into her work.   The semester was over.   A lot of
students were making their way back to their families for the
winter break. Lula stayed on campus working to save some
money.

Chapter 2

The cost of living was very low. The cost of food (apples) were 12 cents a pound. A loaf of bread was 7 cents, and a dozen of eggs were 34 cents. A person who worked an average of 40 plus hours would earn $12.98 a week. A year's salary would be around $574.96.   Now if you only worked 20 hours a week, you would only be earning $6.00 a week. One day, Lula went to the market to get a few things that she needed for herself. She had a hand basket to gather eggs, a loaf of bread, body soap (10 cents a bar), and some rock candy that she really loved as it was very good. As Lula was all ready to check out, she noticed someone behind her. Lula didn't look right away. This person was a man, she could see. His shoes were dress shoes, wool pants, a white shirt with suspenders, and a vest with a boxed bow tie, As Lula turned around and looked up, she made eye contact with the man.   Well, hello said the man. Yes, it was Henry Nixon.   Lula said, "Hello." Henry said, "How have you been?" Lula said, "I'm doing well." "Thank you. "Henry said, "Well that is great." Lula put her things on the counter to pay for them. The storeowner rang her things up. She made her exit out of the door. On her way out she said, "Good seeing you." Henry said, "you as well." Walking down the stairs, she made her way to her dorm, the female hall that only female honor students with "A" averages lived. As she was carrying her bags, the professor asked if he could help her with her bags by offering her a ride. Her walk was about 2 miles. Lula said, "Yes."   Henry helped her into the car, a Ford Model F. It resembled a buggy and had a hood over the seat of the car. But if it was raining, you would still get wet. During the ride taking Lula to her dorm room, they talked about Christmas as it was soon coming. The town was decorated with Christmas festivities. Henry changed the subject He said, "You know I really miss seeing you in class. You know, you're like a ray of sunshine." "You really brighten up my day." Lula looked over to Henry with the biggest smile on her face. Lula's hand was on the seat. Henry slid his hand over to her hand and held her hand until they arrived at her dorm.   Henry asked if he could help her with her things and walk her to the door. Lula said, "Yes, thank you." She opened the door and said to Henry, "Please, please come in. Henry went in and asked Lola should I close the door behind me? Lula said, "Yes, please close the door. May I offer you a cool drink?" Henry said, "Yes, thank you."   Lula brought a glass of tea from the other room for Henry. He took a few sips from the glass and sat it down. He walked toward Lula and put his hand under her chin and kissed her. Lula kissed him back with much compassion. You could hear Lula gasp for air with a slight quiver on her lips. She had never gone this far with anyone, other than Henry. Henry rubbed her face and looked in her eyes. He said to Lula, "I want you." "I need you" as Henry took the bobby pins out of her long thick black hair.   Her hair fell down past her shoulder.   Henry leaned in and smelled her hair. He said, "Your hair smells pretty" rubbing his hand through her hair. Pulling her to him, kissing her all over her face, Lula turned her back to Henry. Henry asked her, do you want me? Lula said, "yes, and Henry helped her unbutton her dress. Her dress fell to the floor. Henry took off his shirt and then his pants. As Henry turned to Lula, he couldn't believe his eyes. Lula was standing there, her hair flowing softly on her shoulders as the light glistened on her Carmel colored skin. Henry walked over to her and kissed her on her face. He rubbed his face against her face. He kissed her on her neck, then her shoulder as they stood in the middle of the room. There was a bed in the room and Lula made her way over to it. She walked back and held Henry's hand. She couldn't ignore his body. She had never seen a man's body without clothes on. His body looked like a bronzed statue or a strong black cup of coffee. She could see that Henry was excited with her. Lula whispered to him, I'm a virgin.   He asked her, do you want me to stop?   Looking at Henry, Lula said, "NO, NO.   They both lay on the bed. Henry and Lula were all caught up in a very long night of passion. Henry was mesmerized by Lula's beauty. They made love over and over. This went on all night long. Lula and Henry started making love around four o'clock pm and fell asleep in each other's arms around three o'clock am. Waking up at the crack of dawn, Henry stared at Lula saying, "You are amazing." Feeling good, Lula smiled. They kissed and made love again.   Henry was feeling so good, but told

Lula that he had some work at the university to tend to.   Henry had gotten dressed and told Lula that he would see her later on in the week.   Henry also said to Lula, "You know that we have to keep what happened between the two of us a secret because of my position at the college and I can lose my job."   Lula said to Henry, "I understand. I would never do anything like that."   "Your secret is safe with me."   She asked Henry, "Will we see each other again?" He said, "Why yes, I want you in my life. "   Things for me right now are a little difficult.   I mean with my job.   I will call you soon. Okay?"   Lula said, "Okay" not being sure of the professor's intentions.   She gave him the phone number to the dorm hall, the only phone in the hallway that everyone on the floor shared.   Henry said to Lula, "you are so beautiful" and held her face in his hand and softly kissed her on her lips as he opened the door and said goodbye.

Later on that week after working hard, Lula had made it home from a long day at work.   Unwinding, lying back in her bed, she thought about how her week had been.   She not only thought about how her week had been, but also about the upcoming semester and the new year that was fast approaching.   On the way into her dorm hall room, she had noticed a flyer.   In the city of Jackson Mississippi, there was juke joint called The Real Delta Blues House. Lula was thinking like WOW!   Listening to some of the music on the radio.   Yes, Lula was dancing around the room feeling good thinking about what had happened this past week, how Henry Nixon was all up in her mind.   Christmas was fast approaching!   She was thinking about what she was going to wear to the New Year Celebration.   I need myself a new hat Lula said, also a new dress.   Lula went over to where she kept her money in her dresser drawer. She was good at saving her money because she was always working.   She would only buy things that she needed, not things that she wanted.   She was really feeling pretty good about herself.   She felt like she had become a woman now.   She thought about making love for her very first time and got caught up in her feelings noticing that flowers are so pretty.

Lula had gathered up her things, as she wanted to do some shopping before the new year came.

Chapter 3

Now it was a few days before Christmas and Lula was getting a few things on top of her shopping list for that new out fit and her new hat.   She was down town looking at some of the dresses that were in the storefront window.   Not seeing anything that she liked, Lula walked over to the next two stores and in the window of one store was the dress that CAUGHT HER EYE!   "WOW" she said, "yes, I want that dress."   It was short sleeved, had glitter on it that was shining.   The hat was more of a band around the head that had a feather sticking out of it.   Lula went into the store and bought the dress and band for her hair.   She was, oh so very EXCITED!

A few days later, it was Christmas and Lula was all alone.   She didn't go home to Alabama.   There were others that also didn't go home.   I guess it was a way to save money.   So everyone in her dorm that didn't go home came together and shared this special day, the Birth Of Christ singing songs, even eating dinner with each other.   That day was a very peaceful day!   Lula had gotten closer to some of the others that were in her dorm hall.   She met a friend that she had been saying hi to as she would come and go through out her day.

They had gotten a little more closer on Christmas Day, confiding in each other.   This new friend's name was Olivia.   Lula had shared with Olivia the New Year's Eve Celebration that was going on in Jackson at The Real Delta Blues House.   She told Olivia about her plans and was so excited during their conversation.   The day had gone by and she was all alone in her room dancing around.   She heard KNOCK, KNOCK, KNOCK!   Lula opened up the door thinking that it was Olivia.   When she opened up the door, much to her surprise, it was Henry!   Henry Nixon!   He said, "Merry Christmas."   Lula said, "Why thank you, and Merry Christmas to you also."   Henry asked can I come in? Lula said, "Well I'm not really supposed to have anyone in my room! "   "I know that you were here before, but that just happened." Henry went in and told Lula, I thought about you all day. I miss you so much. I really can't get you off of my mind. Lula said, "Yeah! "Really?" Henry walked a little closer to her, turned her around with his arms around her as the radio was playing the song "Silent Night" (By The Haydn Quartet). Henry put his face by her face and rocked her side by side, holding her tight. Lula felt as if she would melt. When the song was over, Henry turned her around and looked her in her face. Henry said "I want to make love to you", "I want to feel you", "I need to feel your body." "Lula, baby, do you feel where I'm coming from?" "Don't you want to feel me inside of you?" "Do you love me?" "Do you?" Lula looked at Henry and said to him as her voice was trembling with passion, "yes" Henry, I want you." Henry turns to make sure the door was locked. Henry stepped out of his shoes. He pulls down his suspenders and unzips his pants. Henry was standing there with nothing on but his socks and under wear. Lula was also standing there. He said to her, "I want to watch you undress." "Lula when I look at you I get so excited." "I just want to sit back and look at your beautiful body." Lula had help unbuttoning her dress! As she was standing there, Henry said, "oh my goodness." "Baby I think I could be with you forever." Lula turned around and Henry asked her a question. He said to Lula, "come here" and reached his hand out for Lula as he pulled her close to him. Lula leaned over and started to kiss Henry. Henry just loved her hair. Her hair was pinned up. While they were kissing, Henry started taking her hair down. He was all into the heat of passion. Lula stopped and said, "I can't do this." "I know that we already made love to one another the last time that we were together, but I don't even know you, but yet I want you!" "What are we doing?" "I'm sorry; I can't do this right now!" "Not like this." Lula became a little irate. Her voice had gotten louder. "The last time we were together you disappeared after making love to me." Henry said, "Please, please calm down!" "Lula let me hold you." "I want to bond with you." "I want to one day be your everything." "Please come here so I can hold you in my arms." "I'm not here for sex only." "I want to build a life with you." Henry held out his hand and pulled Lula very close to him. He kissed her on her ear as he began to sing sweet nothing in her ear. Henry said, "You feel so good in my arms." Henry and Lula fell asleep in each other's arms. Henry woke up and started to get dressed while Lula was still asleep. He leaned over and kissed Lula. She was fast asleep and not moving. He peeked out the door to see if there was anyone out there to see him leaving. He walked slowly, making his way out of the dorm, driving away in his car parked down the street.

Morning had come and Lula was still in bed, feeling like a queen. She woke up reaching out for Henry, only to find out that he wasn't there. Looking up at the ceiling, she wondered why would he leave her like that. Going over to the desk, she found a note that Henry left for her telling her "I had to take care of some business." "I kissed you goodbye." I couldn't wake you, you were so beautiful. I didn't want to disturb your sleep. Kisses see you soon." "Henry." Lula laid there for about an hour thinking about how Henry made her feel. She was telling herself that she was in love. Getting herself ready for the day, she made a list of things for the new year to come. The school semester would be here soon and she would have to get her classes and books ready, making sure everything would be in place. She also thought about the New Year's Eve Party, not knowing how she was going to make it to Jackson Mississippi. It was about 75 miles away from where she lived, in Lorman Mississippi. After hanging around the dorm, Lula ran into her friend, Olivia, talking to her about the party once again. Olivia said, "I have family who lives in Jackson and Vicksburg. Let me call them and ask if its okay fur us to come and visit. I will get back with you later on today." Lula said, "Okay, thanks."

Later that day, Olivia had gotten back with Lula letting her know that her family said it was okay for them to visit them on New Year's Eve. So Lula was so excited, jumping up and down Lula and Olivia started making plans because they only had a few days to pull this together.

The next morning, Lula and Olivia had gotten up and called to see how much it would cost for the train ride to Jackson. They called the train station. The person on the other end of the phone told them that it would cost $12.00 a person. Yes, that would be round trip. "Okay" said Lula. Can we pay before we board? The nice person said "yes." For the next two days, Olivia and Lula were very excited with their plans to travel. They were getting their things all together, packing.

December the 29th, they were all packed up, at the train station, dressed up with their big hats and white blouses on, with burgundy long skirts with big petticoats, dress boots that tied all the way up the ankle. Oh, of course, they had on long wool coats. The weather was a bit cool at that time of the year. Now that they had their tickets in their hands, the conductor yelled out "train going to Jackson. All Aboard!" The conductor grabbed Lula's hand and helped her up on the train. They found themselves a seat. 1905 was also the year that a number of Black Activists came together, led by W. E. B. D Bois. William Edward Burghandt Du Bois, an American sociologist, socialist, historian, civil rights activist, Pan-African author, writer, and editor, was born February 23, 1868 in Great Barrington, MA. A Harvard University graduate, Du Bois believed that education was very important in the lives of Black people. He also thought that the country should get rid of segregation.

There were a lot of white people on the train who were looking at the two women with a look of disgust, not wanting to sit with the colored people. Never the less, Lula and Olivia enjoyed each other's company. They were amazed at the view of the countryside. On the way to Jackson, the train stopped from city to city. People were exiting and boarding the train. Arriving in Jackson, the conductor yelled out, "City of Jackson Mississippi." Lula and Olivia's eyes got so big! Big with excitement. The train stopped and the conductor stepped out, so that they could step down off the train. The train was there for a minute, so everyone getting off, could claim their luggage. After getting their luggage and things together, Olivia looked down the walkway outside the train station. There was her auntie and uncle. Auntie Seal and Uncle Willie Earl were very good and God-fearing people. You could see the love that they had for one another. Olivia, her aunt, and uncle, showed Lula nothing but love. They showed her that she was considered to be a new family member in their eyes. Lula showed them nothing but respect. Aunt Seal showed them where they would be sharing a room while staying with them. Aunt Seal had cooked some fried chicken, corn on the cob, mashed potatoes, sun- made ice tea, and homemade apple pie. Everyone were sitting at the table. Uncle Willie started with prayer, thanking the Lord for his family and how blessed he was, and for the meal that was placed before them. Everyone said, "Amen." Everyone enjoyed the meal, talking about everything from school to Lula's family, to church. Dinner was over with Olivia and Lula helping to clean up the kitchen. The kitchen was finally cleaned up. The weather was a little cool, but nice considering it was December. Sitting in the living room listening to the radio, was the entertainment. Lula and Olivia were enjoying the day and the night was fast approaching. As they got ready for bed, Lula said to Olivia, "thank you for showing me a good time."

On the morning of December 30th, Aunt Seal got up cooking breakfast for the ladies. Lula was thinking that she could get used to her new parents, because she wasn't close to her parents. She never really spoke about them. At breakfast, Aunt Seal was telling them about the church service. And how to bring in the new year with the Lord. Aunt Seal said that she wanted them to attend the service. The name of this church was Good Hope Baptist Church; it was a small church where they attended in the area of Jackson and Vicksburg Mississippi. Good Hope would be open this coming Sunday and Monday. It would be a new year. Aunt Seal said, "I pray that God will see us through this New Year." She was shouting "thank you Jesus! " "Thank you."   Later on that day, Lula was asking Olivia how was she going to be able to go to the juke joint? She told her that was the reason that she had come to Jackson. Olivia said, "Yes, it was."   So after the both of them started contemplating, Lula said, "Oh, we will go to the church." "We will come back here and sneak out while they (Aunt Seal and Uncle Willie Earl) are sleep." Olivia said, "Okay, sounds good."

December 31st 1905 was on a Sunday. This day was like the day before. Everyone was getting things in order for the new year, making sure clothes were washed and cleaned, the house cleaned, and helping Aunt Seal with whatever she needed. Aunt Seal seemed very pleased with Lula and Olivia being there with her. The day was coming to an end. Uncle Willie Earl was getting his truck ready for the New Year Celebration. Lula and Olivia sat in the back of the truck while Uncle Willie Earl and Aunt Seal were inside of the church. They made it to church that evening. The other families and members were all gathered in the church. Aunt Seal had taken Lula and Olivia around to meet and introduce them to some of the young ladies who attended the church. Some of the young ladies were the same age as they were. Aunt Seal held her head up being so proud. She told some of the other members, "Hi, these are my nieces, Olivia and Lula." They had met Beatrice and her sister, Big Susan as they called her, and her brother, Miles. They all had the last name Draper. Also at the church was a very nice couple who attended the church. Their names were Martha and Frank Newton. Olivia and Lula smiled and everyone took their places. The church had gotten their praise on singing, shouting, thanking God for keeping their children safe. They embraced the New Year and brought it in praising God.

Chapter 4

January 1906   Happy New Year!

Church was over.   Olivia and Lula were on their way back to Aunt Seal's place.   They could see off the road the Junk Joint that they wanted to attend.   You could hear them, as they were indeed loud. Some of the music was ragtime and some was down home blues. Aunt Seal, Uncle Willie Earl, Lula, and Olivia made it back to the house.   Everyone was tired, so they all went to bed.   Lula and Olivia had gotten up and dressed after pretending to be sleep.   They put pillows in the bed to make it look as if they were there, just in case anyone checked on them throughout the night.   They made their way to the Junk Joint, which was about a mile away.   They only had the moon light to see where they were going.   Yes, they were afraid, yet also determined to go and have some fun. They were also guided by the sound of music. They finally made it to the door of the Juke Joint.   Opening up the door, their eyes were opened wide as they had never been to a place like this before.   Men and women were dancing with their bodies close rocking back and forth to the music.   They were seeing people drinking out of mayonnaise jars. They were drinking what is called Home Made Moon Shine.   Yes, it is said that it is full of spirits, making one feel good or do something that they wouldn't normally do as they were having a good time.   Lula and Olivia had a lot of men heads turned looking at them.   The women there weren't very happy either.   Most of them, (everyone) were there with their own wife or husband.   A few people were there by themselves.   Lula and Olivia went and sat down at a table.   The junk Joint looked like the inside of a person's house.   Enjoying the music, Lula was looking across the room. She thought that she saw Henry, the professor. Yes, Professor Henry Nixon.   Lula couldn't help noticing that he was sitting all hugged up with a woman.   WOW! Lula said to herself.   Lula leaned over to Olivia and told her who Henry was.   Lula felt so hurt, not believing that he never told her anything about his outside life, knowing that she was madly in love with him.   The music was bumping and Lula was asked if she wanted to dance by a man that was looking at her from across the room.   Lula said "yes!" He took her hand and led her to the middle of the floor. Feeling the beat of the music, they were rocking, waving their hands, and snapping their fingers. They were really enjoying themselves. She had met someone to entertain her as well. After about an hour of this, it was getting very hot. Lula and Olivia went outside to get themselves some air. Standing outside, Lula felt someone tap her on her shoulder. She turned around and yes, it was Henry. Henry said "Hi!" Lula said "HI" also. Henry said, "I'm surprised to see you here." He asked Lula, "What are you doing here?" I'm here visiting my family, Lula said. She asked Henry who the woman was that he was sitting with. Henry looked at Lula and spoke with a stern voice saying, "That's my wife." Lula had the moon shining on her face with tears in her eyes. She softly said, "Oh Really?" Henry said, "It's not what you think." "Trust me." We will work something out. The school semester starts on Monday the 8th of next week, and I will see you soon. Olivia and Lula were standing close by each other. Henry's wife walked outside to the door and called his name. She said, "Henry, I was just wondering if you were alright." She asked who the women were that he was talking to Henry said that he was just making conversation with two very nice young ladies. He also told his wife that he was ready to go home. While grabbing his wife's hand, he said to Lula and Olivia, "you ladies have a Happy New Year!" Henry helped his wife into his car and they went on their way. Lula was hurt and didn't really believe what had just happened to her. She couldn't enjoy the rest of the New Year celebration. She asked Olivia if they could just go home to Aunt Seal's house. Olivia said "yes." Lula and Olivia made it back to the house safely. Lula got in bed pulling the cover over head, crying herself to sleep. Olivia got up late that morning of January 1, 1906. She tried to sleep, but she couldn't really sleep well. The sun was shining bright in the room, waking them both up. They made their way in the other room where Aunt Seal was cooking breakfast the hot coffee was smelling good. Aunt Seal was making everyone a plate, talking about their plans for the New Year. Lula and Olivia prepared to leave going back to school at Alcorn University. Lula was thinking to herself, wow did I have Henry all wrong? Aunt Seal said to Lula repeating herself about four times, "Baby where are you?" Lula started to cry. Aunt Seal said to Lula, "it's going to be alright." Aunt Seal enjoyed the girls being there for the rest of the week.

The girls took the train back to Lorman Mississippi. Getting back to the dorm room, they went their own separate ways, preparing themselves to get into their classes and work flow. Lula would work very hard for the next three months, picking up extra days. She worked in the kitchen as a dishwasher and a food prep tech making salads, cutting cake, etc. She also focused on her studies.

One bright sunny day in March of 1906, Lula was into her classes, keeping up with her studies. She was walking to the library to do her homework. She could also relax and unwind there. She had been going there all year not really paying attention as she had gone to get a book from the shelf, upon her return; she noticed a note on top of another book that was in front of her.   The note said, "Hi." "My name is Jonathan E. Brooks." "I think that you are so beautiful, and I was wondering if I could get the chance to know you." After reading the note, Lula looked up to see a very handsome man across the room. He was nicely dressed with black trousers, a nice white shirt with a vest, and a jacket coat hanging over the chair. This man had a smile that could light up a room. His eyes were very big and dreamy, very mesmerizing. He had a head full of cold black hair with waves. Lula was taken back by his presence. All she could do was smile. She went back to doing what she was doing trying to stay cool without showing Jonathan that she very excited about him. She kept looking up from time to time, looking at Jonathan with a very half smile, blushing and being somewhat bashful. This time, when Lula looked up, standing almost over her, was Jonathan. The young man said "Good afternoon. Please let me formally introduce myself" as he took Lula's hand and kissed it very softly. He said, "My name is Jonathan Edwards Brooks and I'm very pleased to meet you." Lula said to Jonathan, "the feeling is mutual." My name is Lula Hood." Jonathan said, "You are like a beautiful flower. I really can't take my eyes off of you. May I please have the pleasure of getting to know you? Lula was in a frozen state for a moment, but then said, "Okay, yes, that would be nice. Jonathan said "can we do lunch or maybe dinner? Lula was really at a loss for words for a minute.   She had never really been asked out for a date before. She gave him the phone number to the dorm where she was living. Lula didn't want him to know exactly where she lived. Jonathan took her number and went on his way.   Before he left, he turned and gave Lula the biggest smile, which made her day.

Making it back to her dorm with her books in her arms, Lula runs into Olivia.   She said, "Oh my, I met this very handsome man." Yelling with excitement, "HE ASKED ME OUT or well not yet, but he asked me for my number."   Olivia and Lula were jumping up and down with joy!   Later on that night, another person that was in the dorm knocked on the door. The young lady said to Lula, "you have a phone call." The phone was at the end of the hallway so that everyone could share it. It was on a table that had two chairs. Lula thanked the young lady and made her way to the phone. She picked it up with the receiver to her ear and picked up the part to talk into. She said "hello."   The person on the other end said, "Hello. Lula, this is Jonathan.   With the biggest smile on her face, Lula said, "Hi Jonathan. How are you?"   He said, "I'm very good.   Thank you for asking."   "You know I told you that I'm very interested in getting to know you and I was wondering if you would consider having dinner with me this coming weekend?   There was a pause and Jonathan said, Lula?   She said, "I'm sorry, "yes, yes I would like that. Jonathan and Lula talked for about 5 more minutes before they ended the phone call. Jonathan said, "I will call you back so I can find out where to pick you up".   Lula asked Jonathan "would it be alright if I could meet you for dinner?" Jonathan said, "Yes that would be fine. Before I go, can I pray for you and for me and that, you will have a blessed night? Lula said, "thank you as they hung up the phone. Getting herself ready for bed that night, Lula took a bath, a bubble bath, relaxing in the tub. Drying herself off, she got ready for bed.

The next morning, on her way to class, Lula runs into Olivia.   "Hi Lula", Olivia said. Lula said 'hi" telling Olivia about her date the coming weekend.   Lula wanted a new look to be very polished.

Olivia agreed with her, telling Lula, "You have always worn your hair so natural. Have you ever heard of the pressing comb?" Lula said, "Yes I heard of this colored woman by the name of Madam C. J. Walker. Her products makes us colored women hair look amazing. Olivia said, "Why you should try it. Your hair is already beautiful." I know the woman that's selling her hair care products and she also has a pressing comb, and it's only $3.00 to get your hair done. "Okay" let's go," said Lula. Olivia got on the phone and called to make an appointment for Lula. Olivia came back to tell Lula that the lady could get her in to her hair later on that day around 6:00 PM. Lula said, "No, that's not going to work." "I have another class today and I'm also scheduled to work tonight." "I'm off tomorrow at 6:00 PM." Please Olivia, can you call back and change my appointment?" "Okay" I will call her back," Olivia said. "I would have called her myself, but she is your friend." "I don't know her," Lula said. Olivia said, "You're right," Olivia said. "I will call her right now." After being gone for about 10 minutes, Olivia returned to tell Lula, "I made your appointment. It is all set. She will see you tomorrow at 6 PM. Lula gave Olivia a real big hug and thanked her at the same time. Lula asked Olivia, "Are you going to go with me?" "I will see." I will try, but you are a big girl" "You don't need me." Lula said, "Yes I do, you're like a sister to me." "Really I feel like as far as family goes, you're all the family I have." Olivia said to Lula, "that's fine, but tell me something." "Why don't you want to talk about your family?" "my mama, well she cleans houses for the white people" My daddy, well, I saw them beat and hang him from a tree" Lula said and began to cry.   Olivia pulled a clean handkerchief out of her purse giving it to Lula saying, "I didn't mean to upset you." "I just wondered because you never talk about your family," Olivia said. "It's okay, it's okay Girl." "I have to get to class." "I will see you tonight or later on."

The next day was pretty much like the day before. Lula had made plans to meet Olivia after she was done with her class at 3:00PM. Olivia was waiting outside of her classroom. There was an area where you could sit and do homework. Lula said, "Let's get something to eat before I go and get my hair done. My treat to you." "That sounds good," "I am so hungry" Olivia said. They started to walk, making made their way to buy burgers at a store called Wool Worth's. There was a counter in this store where you could sit down and place your order. Lula and Olivia sat down at the counter. The man behind the counter said to them, "You niggers know better than to sit down here." "We don't serve your kind in here!" Gone gal, get, get out of here!" Lula and Olivia got up and went on their way. When the ladies were on campus being at an all-black college, they didn't have that problem with segregation like they did when going out into the real world. In the south, you had to say Yes Sir, or "Yes Maa'm to the white people. Lula and Olivia being a little frustrated got their things and left. Lula said to Olivia, "maybe we can go to my hair appointment." They walked to the lady's house. That's how Olivia and Lula got around. Arriving at Olivia's friend's house, they went to the door and began knocking. The lady opened up the door and said, "Hello, come on in." Lula and Olivia stood in the doorway. Olivia said to her friend, "this is Lula" and to Lula, "this is my friend, Mary Alice." Mary Alice invited them both in and they walked to the back of the house. This part of the house was the kitchen. Mary Alice said to Lula, "Olivia told you the price, right?" Lula said, "yes", she said $3.00." "Oh NO! "I'm going to have to charge you $4.00." "I didn't know you had so much hair." Mary Alice was trying to explain when you have a lot of hair that would be extra work for her. Lula said to Mary Alice, "you said it would be $3.00. " "Well I didn't know what I was working with." "Your hair is very long," said Mary Alice. Lula said, "okay"." Mary Alice started washing Lula's hair. After drying her hair with a towel, she used a big comb to detangle her hair, putting her hair in 4 plaits. Mary Alice then placed Lula under a hair dryer. Lula had never had anyone do her hair before, other than her mother. Olivia was sitting making small talk with Mary Alice. They both were talking about the old times, about old friends from both of their pasts. Mary Alice was also checking on Lula's hair. It was time to come from under the hair dryer. Yes, her hair was dry. It was time to take down Lula's hair. Mary Alice was using a hot plate that she would put the metal comb on and it would get hot. Then it would be used to

press out the hair. Mary Alice had gotten halfway done with
Lula's hair. She was not paying attention to what she was doing!
Mary Alice had dropped that hot pressing comb down Lula's back.
Lula jumped up screaming and also hollering from the pain of
being burned. The pressing comb fell out the back of Lula's shirt.
Lula yells out to Mary Alice, "What the heck are you doing?"
Lula had never ever talked like that before.   Olivia said to Mary
Alice, "what are you doing?" "What is this about?" Olivia asked
Lula, "Girl are you alright?" Lula said, "I'm not sure." Olivia
looked at Lula's back. There was a bright red spot on her back.
Mary Alice said to Lula, "I 'm so sorry. Really I am." " Please let
me finish your hair, please." " I really didn't mean for that to
happen." Take a few minutes and get yourself together." " I will
go outside and get myself some air also'. Lula said to herself, "I
knew this heifer was jealous."   Both Mary Alice and Lula took
themselves a 15-minute break. After the break, Lula went back
into the kitchen.   Lula was thinking if this cow burn me one
more time, I'm going to have to tussle with her. Mary Alice had
gotten done with Lula's hair. She gave Lula a mirror so that she
could see herself. Olivia was the first to say 'WOW!" Your
hair is beautiful." Lula was looking in the mirror and was very
pleased with her hair. Lula paid Mary Alice for doing her hair.
Yes, she paid $4.00 despite being burned. Mary Alice walked
both of them to the door, seeing them on their way. Olivia and
Lula walked back to the dorm. On their way back, they talked
about going back to get Lula's hair done again by Mary Alice,
Lula decided that she would give Mary Alice one more chance.
They both went back to their dorm rooms. Lula heard the phone
ring. She had only been there about 5 minutes. There was a
knock at the door. Someone called out Lula, the phone is for
you. Lula said, "I will be right there." Lula went to the
phone and picked up the phone to say, "Hello this is Lula." The
person on the phone said "hi. How are you?" "This is Jonathan I
am calling you to tell you where I made plans for dinner." "I
would like to take you out for dinner. The place that I chose is
called "Estelle's. They cook southern food." " Do you know
where this place is?" Lula said, "I think so. I believe it's off of
Indian Spring Road." Jonathan said, "YES! YES! That's the

place."   Are you sure that you don't want me to pick you up?"
Lula said, "No, I will meet you there." What time should I be
there?"   Jonathan said 6 PM.   Lula said, "okay", I will see you
soon."   They both hung up the phone.
Lula stretched her arms out and did a big twirl feeling good, also
feeling joy.   The phone rang before she made it back to her room.
It was Jonathan.   "I did say this Saturday, didn't I", he asked.
Lula said, "Yes, you did."   Jonathan said, "okay", I will see you
soon."   Both of them said "good Night."

Back in her room, putting things out so that she could decide what
she wanted to wear on her dinner date, Lula selected the dress that
she wanted to wear on her dinner date. She hung the dress on the
back of the door. The shoes and hat that she wanted to wear were
also selected.   Everything was on point.   Now all tired out,
getting herself ready for bed,   Lula was thinking about all the
things that she had experienced since attending college. She
thought about Henry Nixon. It had been a few months since she
had heard from him.   The memories were pulling at her heart.
She remembered hearing Henry saying, "It's not what you think"
and her thinking to herself, "I know that he loves me and I know
that I love him."   She was also thinking, "Why hasn't he gotten
back with me?" He said, "That he would explain everything to
me. "   She felt that thinking of Jonathan might be better for her.
Finally, Lula fell fast asleep.

Chapter 5

It was now Saturday morning.   The sun was shining so bright.
Lula was so excited about her plans for the day.   She had gotten
up, got dressed, and went out the door.   Lula went over to Olivia's
dorm room and knocked on her door.   Olivia asked, "Who is it?"
Lula yelled, "It's me Olivia."   I wanted to know if you wanted to
go over to the cafeteria with me and have breakfast."   Olivia
said, "okay", give me a few minutes and I will be ready."
Lula ran back to her room to get her purse and waited in the
hallway for Olivia.   Olivia came out of her room and told Lula,
"I'm ready."   They both started to walk over to the cafeteria.
They waited in line to place their orders.   They had coffee, juice,
bacon, eggs, grits, and toast for breakfast.   Lula noticed there was
a table not too far away.   Sitting there having breakfast was
Professor Henry Nixon. He looked like he was having a meeting
with some of the other professors conducting business.   Lula was
trying not to look at him.   She continued to eat her breakfast, but
gazed over to take a quick look over in his direction.   Their eyes
locked for a second.   Lula hurried up and looked away with a
bashful look on her face.   Olivia said to Lula, "I know you don't
still have feelings for him."   Lula said, "of course not."   "I have
a date that I need to get ready for tonight.   They continued to
enjoy the meal.   Henry Nixon made his way over to the table
where Lula was sitting.   He walked past her to throw his trash in
the dumpster.   Henry said, "how are you ladies this morning?"
Both ladies just smiled and the professor kept on going.   Lula tried
not to look as he walked on away.   She continued talking to
Olivia.   The ladies had finished their breakfast.   Trying to regroup
herself, Lula walked with Olivia back to their dorm rooms.   "It's
time to re-pin your hair because you have a date tonight", Olivia
said.

Later on that day, Lula had taken a bath and put lotion on her body
so that it wouldn't be ashy.   She put her dress on and it was very
different from what she was used to wearing...   The color was very

stunning as the dress was royal blue. It was made of nylon and very fitting. It complemented her body and came above her ankles. Her shoes were silver. She wore a hat that was pinned up on her hair with silver beads on it and a pearl necklace. She also sprayed on some perfume, smelling very pretty. Lula looked in the mirror and was very happy with her appearance. It was now time to leave for the restaurant. One of her friends who live in the dorm agreed to give her a ride. Olivia also went along for the ride downtown. They left the dorm around 5 PM, as she wanted to be on time. Olivia told Lula that she really looked amazing. Arriving at the restaurant, Lula said, "Thank you" " "Thanks for everything." Olivia answered, "You are so welcome." "That's what friends are for." Lula got out of the car, looking up to make sure that she was in the right place. As she was opening the door, she was greeted with 12-inch long stem roses by Jonathan. Jonathan was dressed very sharp with a gray suit with a silver vest with suspenders. His shoes were black and gray suede Stacy Adams His hair was cold black with waves. Jonathan had big dreamy eyes. Lula was really taken back by the attention that Jonathan was showing her. She was frozen in time for a moment. Jonathan placed Lula's hand in his to guide her to the table that he had reserved. He pulled the chair out for her and helped her to get comfortable. He then went around the table to seat himself. The waiter came over to bring them a menu. Jonathan started talking with Lula asking how her day was going. Lula said that her day was good. Jonathan said, "I see that you attend Alcorn University "and asked what was she majoring in. Lula said, "Well yes, and my major is Education as I plan on being teacher. " Jonathan said, "Wow, I'm sorry for staring at you." "My, you are so beautiful". Lula looked down really bashful, saying, "thank you." "I brought you a vase to put your flower in," said Jonathan. Lula smiled and said "thank you." Jonathan asked her if she would like a soda. She said, "Yes a Coca-Cola please. Jonathan waved his hand to motion the waiter over because they were ready to order their dinner. Lula ordered fried chicken, mashed potatoes, green beans with a coca cola. Jonathan said, "That sounds great, I'll have the same thing." Jonathan said to Lula, "I could look at you all day." Lula smiled and Jonathan asked her to please tell him everything about herself as he was very interested in her.   Lula said, "I came from Alabama, I have 3 brothers. My mom is a very hard worker. My father was killed by… well we found him hanging in a tree. Jonathan said, "I'm very sorry to hear that." "I know that had to be very devastating." "Yes it was", Lula, said. "My daddy was my world." "He would tell me how he wanted better for me." "I have that memory sketched in my mind and soul." Wanting to change the subject, Lula asked Jonathan what he did for a living. Well, I'm a student also, looking to go into law Jonathan said. He added, "My parents are both living here in Mississippi."   They both listened to each other, having an excellent conversation, laughing.   Dinner was over and they prepared to leave.   Jonathan asked if they could go for a walk.   By this time, Lula felt very comfortable with Jonathan. He had a truck parked outside. He said, "I know a place by the river where we can talk a little more." Lula said, NO! "There is a place back at campus where we can sit and talk also. Jonathan asked if she was going to let him know where she lived. Lula said, "yes and no.!" "I will share with you the area; I just need to be sure who you really are. I like you, but a lady can never be too safe."   Jonathan agreed saying, safety is very important and I am a true gentleman. Lula looked and smiled. Jonathan opened up the door for Lula, helping her into the truck. He got in on the other side.   Lula showed Jonathan a place close to her dorm room. They both got out the truck, talking, holding hands, and looking into the sky at the big full moon.   Jonathan looked at Lula and asked her if he could kiss her.   She said', "yes on my cheek."   She felt that on their first date, a kiss on the cheek was only appropriate.   It was getting late and Lula thanked Jonathan for such a wonderful time and also said, "I will see you soon. She walked away, headed for her room.   Jonathan stood there, watching Lula walk away until he could no longer see her. He then left.

Back in her dorm room, Lula placed the vase of flowers on the table.   Looking at, smelling, and admiring them, she walked over to her radio and turned it on. She felt very beautiful. She sang listening to the music. It was getting late and Lula started to undress, standing there with stockings and bra on. As she went to hang her dress up and put it away, someone was tapping and knocking on the door. Thinking nothing of it, opening up the door, she said, "hi Olivia! She walked away from the door; the other person came in and closed the door. "WOW!" Said Henry Nixon! Lula turned around and asked him, "What are you doing here?" PLEASE LEAVE! PLEASE! Henry said, "Baby please let me explain." Lula said you have five minutes to explain to me. Henry told her, the last time I saw you was this morning.   You woke my heart up again. Lula said, "NO! Henry I waited for you and its March now. "I know baby, I know", Henry said. "When you saw me with my wife, I was not happy, and I'm getting a divorce.   I'm not in love with my wife. We have just been going through the motions of being married. I sleep alone on the sofa." "I love you!" "I NEED YOU."   Lula started to cry, saying, 'I LOVE YOU TOO!" She looked very sexy standing there in her bra, panties, and stockings. Henry took a seat at the table holding Lula's hand as she sat on his lap. "Please let me show you how much I missed you", Henry said. "Trust me, things will be different." Henry looked on the table and said, "Those are some beautiful flowers." "What did you do to your hair?" "Something's different about it."   Lula said that the flowers were from a friend, and thanked him. Henry said, "Baby stand up. I want to see what I've been missing." "You know I really missed you, right? "Well, I'm not sure" Lula said. Henry stood up and took his coat off.   Lula asked him, "What are you doing?" Henry asked if she wanted him to leave and started putting his coat back on. Lula said, "wait, wait you're right. I do miss you too."   Henry took his coat off again and sat down in the chair. Music was playing and Lula started dancing. Henry was really enjoying her body, saying, "Yes, yes baby." With all of the silliness going on, Lula fell into Henry's arms. They both looked at each other. Henry held her face in his hands as he gazed into her eyes, not wanting this moment to end. He told her how beautiful she was and kissed her face and then her lips. Lula started to unbutton his shirt and placed her hand on his chest. She could hear and feel his heart beating faster. She stood up, took off her

panties and stockings, standing there nude. Henry took off his
pants standing there nude,   sat back in the chair that he was sitting
in.   He was overcome with the way she looked. Lula sat on
Henry's lap. He touched every inch of her body. She was getting
very loud with the passion of the both of them making love to one
another. Henry was all caught up with the way Lula made him
feel, yelling to the top of his voice with so much excitement. Lula
could feel the professor in her heart. All of this was so
overwhelming for Henry. He yelled out "I can't take it."   "I
need to re-group myself."   Lula got up and went to bed.   Henry
followed her to the bed snuggling up behind her.   Lula laid there
just staring into space,   not really believing that she had fallen for
Henry once again!   Henry asked, "What's wrong?"   Lula said,
"You're what's wrong."   "You know how I feel about you and
you keep playing with my emotions." "Also, you never told me
that you were married!" "You know that really hurt."   "You then
never came back to say anything!"   "I'm just really hurt."
Henry said, "Well I'm not going to lie to you."   "I am only
married on paper."   "I don't have sex with my wife."   "I love
you, I want you baby, I need you."   Henry held Lula by the waist
kissing her on her neck.   He made love to her over and over all
night long.   They fell asleep in each other's arms.   Five AM
came very fast.   Henry woke up telling Lula good-bye.   Lula
said "good-bye sweetie, see you later on,"   Henry said, "yes you
will." Lula went back to sleep. The professor looked out the
door making sure that no one knew that he was there.

It was now Sunday morning and Lula had slept in.   It was noon
before she had gotten up.   Olivia was knocking at her door.
Lula answered the door with a robe on.   Olivia told Lula, okay,
okay, I want to know all about your date.   By the look of it, you
must have had a hell of a date! Lula said, "Well, well, my date
with Jonathan was really sweet" Lula put her head down and
started to cry.   Olivia asked, what, what happened? What did he
do?   Tell me what's wrong.   Lula said, "nothing, it's not
Jonathan..." Olivia said, "Then what's wrong?" We are like
sisters" Lula said, "yes we are." "I just need to rest;   I will

come talk to you tomorrow."   She closed the door, took her robe off, and got back in bed nude feeling all emotional and vulnerable. She was not sure if she even wanted to get up today!   She did know however, that she had to pull herself together   She had classes on Monday and had to work four hours for the next three days.   She also had to work the upcoming weekend.

Chapter 6

Lula made it through the week going to class and working. She
tried to stay busy. It was Wednesday now. Back at her room
doing homework, she could hear the phone ring.   She walked
down the hallway to answer the phone. "Hello Lula, is that you?"
Jonathan asked. "Yes, this is me," Lula said. "This is Jonathan,
He said. Are you alright?" She said, "Hi Jonathan, how are
you?" "I'm fine, just missing you and wanted to know if I could
see you maybe this weekend."   Lula said, "I'm sorry but I have to
work this weekend Saturday and Sunday." Jonathan asked, "Well
what about tomorrow?" I will meet you at the cafeteria,   maybe
for coffee." " I just want to see you". "I want you to meet my
parents." Lula said, "okay, yes I can meet you there after my class
around 3:30. Is that fine?" Jonathan said, "That's fine." "Okay,
I'll see you soon." Lula said, "Good-bye." "Have a very nice
day."   She hung the phone up. Knowing that there was only a
few months left before the end of the semester and that summer
school was fast approaching, she wanted to make sure that she was
concentrating on getting the best grade that she could. Lula spent
the rest of the day catching up on her studies, listening to the radio,
and arranging her things in order for the next day.

Lula started thinking things over. It had been more than four days
since she had seen Professor Henry Nixon. Knowing how he had
done this in the past,   she made it up in her mind that although she
loved Henry, it was time to let go and move on because he was
only playing with her emotions. She prepared herself for school
the next morning knowing that she had three long classes. Having
a lot on her mind, she fell fast asleep.   She dreamed that she was
dressed up in a white wedding dress, walking down the church
aisle getting ready to marry the professor. She dreamed that they
were holding hands saying their vows. As they were getting ready
to kiss, Lula heard the alarm clock going off. RING! Ring!
RING!   Lula lay there for a few minutes before getting up to get

ready for school.   She thought to herself,   why I am dreaming about this 'man?   She brushed her teeth, took a quick Bath, dried herself off, and put on her outfit.   She was now ready to go out the door.   Seeing Olivia, she called out, "hey girl!" "How are you?"   "Hey!" "I'm fine,"   said Olivia.   They walked to class together.   Olivia said, "I'm worried about you."   "Why" said Lula.   Olivia said, "Well it's none of my business, but I know that you and Jonathan went out on your first date this past Saturday and everyone could hear you making it out."   "The funny thing is you could hear Jonathan moaning and really expressing himself." "Girl, I see you have a lot of skills."   "You were really putting it on him."   Lula smiled and didn't say a word.   Olivia asked Lula if she wanted to go to town just to hang out after class.   Lula told her that she was meeting Jonathan to have coffee and asked Olivia if she would like to come along.   "OH NO"   said Olivia.   "I would be laughing at him too hard."   "You can ask Jonathan if he has a brother, cousin, or friend."   'I sound a little desperate, don't I?"   Lula said, "OH, NO!"   "I will ask him though."   Olivia said, "Girl, I want to put something down on a brother."   Hell I might hurt the poor man."   "I sure will tell him," Lula said.   She laughed as they parted and went their separate ways.   Making it to class, Lula couldn't help to think,   "Man, was I that loud that everyone could hear me and the professor?"   She couldn't tell Olivia that it wasn't Jonathan that she was with.

The day was long and it was now time for lunch.   Not wanting to eat anything heavy, Lula had some soup as she had one more class before 3:30.   Making it to her last class of the day, she sat by two other young ladies who were holding a conversation about how sexy Professor Nixon was.   Lula listened very closely,   over hearing how the professor was sweet on one of them.   She heard one of the girls telling the other one how he had brushed the side of her face and kissed her.   Lula's heart felt like it had dropped out of her chest.   She tried to concentrate on her class.   When the class was over, she sat there in her chair.   The teacher called out to her saying, "Lula. Lula, class is over."   "Oh, oh, I'm sorry."   "My mind was somewhere else."   Making her way to meet with

Jonathan, her mind was on Henry. It was 3:30fPM and Lula was standing in the cafeteria looking around for Jonathan. She didn't see him. As she turned around', he was walking toward her. He greeted her with his bright smile and said, "I'm so sorry that I'm late." "Oh, that's okay, just got here," said Lula. Jonathan said, "Hi beautiful." "How was your day?" "You made my day." "My day was kinda long." "Please tell me how I made your day." "Well, where should I start?" "Lula, I love the way that you carry yourself, you have so much class and grace about yourself." "Your smile is like a ray of sunshine and any man should be so honored to have you as his wife. "I'm going to hopefully marry you one day if you give me that chance. Lula looked with this I can't believe it look on her face, thinking I fell for the professor and should have been thinking about how Jonathan had shown me such a beautiful time on the first date and WOW! He said, "He wants to marry me." "Jonathan walked Lula to the table and pulled out her seat for her.   He told Lula, I want to get to know you more. Please hold on. Let me get you something to drink. Would you like something to eat? Please excuse me; I'm getting a little nervous.   You see the effect you have on me.   Lula smiled at Jonathan and asked if she could have a cup of coffee and some French fires.   Jonathan said, "Anything you want."   He walked over to place their order and came back with their drinks and food. He placed the coffee and food down carefully and sat down. He told Lula, I want you as my wife and I want to provide and protect you. He also jumped up with a loud voice saying, "I want to profess my true undying love for you." "I want you to meet my parents." Lula sat there speechless. Jonathan asked her, "Well what do you think about that Lula?"   Lula said, "I want to get to know you too." "I would love all of that, I just don't know you well enough to marry you." "I would like to have a courtship with you and get to know you better.'" "Is that okay?" "I want to be sure." "Building a relationship takes a lot of time. "It's like a melting pot," said Jonathan.   "We will build on it together and in this pot I'm adding my ingredients. They are trust, honesty, loyalty, and God! God is the one main ingredient that we should always use first and foremost.   Lula really got into the conversation, as it was deep and said, "I have some ingredients

too! She said her ingredient was compassion and that it allows
each other to be cherished and have love for each other.   Lula and
Jonathan were all wrapped up in each other and lost track of the
time.   Jonathan asked Lula if he could walk her to her dorm and
she said, "Yes" I would like that" and I have a friend named Olivia
and she wants to know if you could introduce her to one of your
friends or someone."   "Okay, I have a roommate named Oscar and
will ask him to see if he is interested.   Maybe we can go out
together on a double date.   What do you think about that?   Lula
was just smiling saying, "that would be great."   They walked
back to Lula's dorm holding hands.   Jonathan carried Lula's
books. As they approached the dorm, Olivia and a few others were
sitting out having conversations.   The ladies started to giggle.
Lula said, "Hi Olivia, I would like for you to meet my friend,
Jonathan.   Olivia looked Jonathan up and down saying, "I'm very
pleased to meet you" as he shook her hand.   Olivia said "yes" it's
very nice to meet you."   Lula told Olivia that Jonathan might
have a friend for her to meet and that his name was Oscar.   Olivia
told Lula that that sounded very nice and that she was looking
forward to meeting him.   Jonathan walked Lula to her room and
nervously asked if he could kiss her good night.   She said, "yes"
I would like that" and they kissed each other.   Jonathan was
taken back by their kiss saying to Lula, 'WOW!' "It's everything
that I could imagine." Lula smiled and they kissed again.
Jonathan felt himself getting excited.   Lula stepped back because
she could feel Jonathan's body change through their kiss.
Jonathan said, "Please forgive me."   Lula kissed Jonathan one last
time. This time, Lula was all caught up in the passion forgetting
who she was kissing. For one quick second, her mind wondered
off to the kiss that she that she had shared with the professor.
Jonathan jumped back, not that he didn't enjoy it.   Jonathan didn't
want to push Lula away. He said, "My, that was very nice."
When can I see you again?" "Hold up."   "I need to clear
something up."   "You are my girl, right?" Lula smiled and said to
Jonathan, "yes you're my beau."   "So I'm your boyfriend and you
think that I'm handsome too?" Jonathan asked. Lula smiled as
she opened the door and said "good night" to Jonathan on the other
side of the door.   They could feel each other as she leaned on the

door smiling. Both said 'WOW!" Jonathan walked away passing
Olivia and the other ladies with some joy in his heart.   He said,
"good night", you ladies have a very good night" and walked
away.

Lula was back in her room thinking Wow!   I have a boyfriend as
she danced around the room with so much joy and happiness.   It
was getting late and she was getting ready for her weekend having
to work Saturday and Sunday.   The next morning Lula was
working in the cafeteria. She went out to clean the tables, clean
the plates and dishes out for the breakfast crowd.   She also
prepared food for those coming for lunch, which included small
salads, doughnuts, cakes.   She also sat the tables with dishes and
silver ware. She also washed dishes.   Lula saw Henry Nixon
enjoying the company of some of his colleagues.   She pretended
that he wasn't there,   completing her busy schedule.   As Henry
finished his breakfast, he walked over to Lula on his way out of the
cafeteria and said, "Hi pretty lady."   Lula pretended NOT TO
HEAR HIM.

Later on that day before her shift ended in about 30 minutes. Lula
was finishing up in the dining area.   She was carrying things into
the kitchen.   When she returned to the dining area, Jonathan was
standing there saying, "hi sweetheart."   "I came to see if I could
walk you home from work."   Lula smiled at Jonathan saying,
"Mr. Brooks, I would love it."   I get off in about 30 minutes."
Jonathan said, "Okay I will sit over here and wait for you."   Lula
smiled and went back to work.   Lula walked from the kitchen
area to where Jonathan was sitting after 30minutes and told him,
"I'm all done."   Jonathan got up from his chair and asked Lula if
he could carry her things for her. She said, "yes" thank you
Jonathan."   Jonathan said, "can we go somewhere for something
to drink?' I mean I don't want this time to end with you."   Lula
said, "I look a mess."   Jonathan said, "Sweetie, you look
amazing to me."   I just want to talk.   Lula said "okay."   They
both ended up on a bench that was on campus.   They sat and
talked for hours laughing and sharing their hopes and dreams.

Jonathan sat with his arms around Lula.   It was after six PM and Lula said, "Well, it's time for me to turn in."   "I have to get up and go to work tomorrow.   Jonathan said, "Okay, I will walk you to your dorm."   Lula said, "yes" I would like that."   They held hands as they walked to Lula's room.   Getting to the door,   Lula turned to Jonathan and said, "good night" and they kissed and exchanged a big hug.   Lula told Jonathan that she was tired and just wanted to rest.   Jonathan understood and told her that he would see her tomorrow.   Jonathan and Lula spent time seeing and getting to know each other almost every day for the next four weeks.

Chapter 7

Lula was up in the morning of April 18, 1906 not feeling well. She was in the bathroom vomiting and not feeling up to par. She laid back in her bed, got back up going to the bathroom vomiting again, not being able to keep anything on her stomach. She sat there for a moment. Her face was very flush, her forehead sweating. Feeling exhausted, Lula was going to class. But she thought that, well maybe I should stay home, as she didn't know what was wrong. She had some saltine crackers on the table and started eating them. Still not feeling well enough to make it to class, Lula decided to stay home to rest. Lying in bed listening to the radio, there was some breaking news. The announcer stated San Francisco located on the west coast in northern California, had had a 7.9 magnitude earthquake, Over 3,000 people were killed. The earthquake started at 5:12 AM central mountain time on Wednesday, April 18, 1906. There was mass devastation. There was a knock at the door. It was Olivia. She asked from the other side of the door, "Did you hear about the earthquake?" Lula opened up the door and said, "Yes, I'm listening to the news now!" Olivia went in and sat on the bed with Lula. They both listened to the news for the rest of the day, which held their attention until later on that night.

Later on that night, Lula turned to Olivia and told her that she needed to see a doctor as she hadn't been feeling well, hadn't had her period that month and should have had it two weeks ago, and had been throwing up all morning. Olivia's eyes got real big and she asked Lula if she and Jonathan were having a baby. Lula got very quiet. She said, "You know when you said that you heard noise coming from my room the night that Jonathan and I had gone out, well it wasn't Jonathan." Olivia said, 'WHAT?" "WHAT DO YOU MEAN?" "Well, who was it?" Lula put her head down and looked up very slowly. Olivia said, "Please don't say what I think you're going to say!" Lula said, "Well I was with the professor that night." "I wish that it wasn't true. Olivia said,

"Hold on.   Do you mean to tell me that it was Professor Nixon?"
"Yes, I don't know what to do" Lula said. Olivia said, "Well you
don't know if you're pregnant for sure.   We'll find a doctor in the
area first.   I will ask around for you and let you know something
in the morning.   Get yourself some rest."   Lula said, "Okay."
The next morning Lula had gotten ready for class to keep her
normal schedule.   As she walked out of her dorm heading to her
first class, Jonathan was waiting to walk her to class.   He told her
that he had looked for her the day before and wanted to know if
everything was okay.   He said, "You know I had missed you."
Lula told him that she had a very bad headache, needed to rest, and
that was the only problem.   She also told him that she stayed in as
she always wanted to look and feel her very best.   Jonathan told
her that on her worst day, she would still be the most beautiful
woman in the world to him.   She looked at him with a big smile
and blushed.   Jonathan asked her for her plans for the weekend.
She said, "Well, I don't have to work.   Other than homework,
I'm fee."   Jonathan told her that he had talked with his roommate
Oscar and that he wanted to meet Olivia.   Lula asked, "What do
you have in mind?"   Jonathan stated that there would be a
luncheon; the speaker would be Booker T. Washington, he had
four tickets, and he thought that it would be a very nice first date
for Oscar and Olivia.   He also mentioned that being a Black
American and leader, he enjoyed learning about Black educators.
He also said, "Booker T. Washington believes that the only way
to freedom is through education."   He also asked Lula if she knew
that Booker T. Washington was born into slavery and made his
way to freedom.   Lula told him that the luncheon would be
marvelous and that she would inform Olivia.   Jonathan said,
"Okay" the luncheon will be this Saturday. I will pick you up at
noon. I know that there will be a very large crowd, so we want to
get there early and get good seats."   He also asked if she would
like to have dinner with him and his parents on Sunday.   She said,
"yes" that she would be honored to have dinner with them."
Jonathan told Lula that he would wait for her after class if she
wanted him to.   She told him that she had made plans to meet
with Olivia around 3:30 PM and that she could see him around
6:00 PM. Jonathan said, "Okay, I will see you then.   She told

him to have a BLESSED DAY!   Jonathan turned, looked at her, and said, "I have already been blessed today with your presence.   I will see you soon my love."   They both gave each other a good-bye kiss and went their separate ways.

Later on that day, Lula was sitting on a bench outside on campus waiting patiently for Olivia.   She looked around wondering where she could be.   Olivia walked down the corridor and they both waved at each other.   Lula asked Olivia about her day and what had she found out about doctors in the area.   Olivia said, "My day was fine. How are you feeling?"   Lula told her that her day was also fine and that she felt okay, but felt a little nervous. Olivia informed her that there was a clinic on Jefferson Street that she had called and pretended to be her,   and that she made an appointment for her on Monday at 11:00 Am.   She also told her that she would go with her and that the name of the clinic was South Central located adjacent to the hospital.   Lula thanked her saying "you know I've never been sick before and I don't even have a doctor."   Olivia assured her that she would be there for her. Lula thanked her again.   She also told Olivia that she had spoken to Jonathan earlier in the day and that he wanted her to ask her if she would be interested in going to a luncheon to hear Booker T. Washington speak and that his roommate, Oscar, would like to meet her.   She also mentioned that he had four tickets and that they all could attend.   She asked Olivia what she thought about these plans and if she would like to go.   Olivia asked, "What, what is his name?" What does he look like?" Yes, I want to go said Olivia.   "Well, good"" said Olivia.   I will let Jonathan know later on tonight. I will see him at 6:00 PM.   Olivia asked Lula if she knew anything about Jonathan's roommate.   Lula explained that she didn't know much about him except that his name was Oscar and that if she didn't like him, it was just a luncheon.   She also told Olivia that she wouldn't be forced to be with him and that she could end the date after the luncheon.   Olivia said, "oh okay, that sounds good." "I hope he is handsome." "I see that he must be educated." "That is a good thing."   She also told Lula, I'm not trying to pry into your business, but I see that you and Jonathan are getting very close. So, what are you going to do if you're pregnant? "Well I really don't know yet," said Lula. "I'm going to take one day at a time because I can't lose Jonathan. He is my world. He shows me what love is all about. He is never quick to anger. Never boasts, he is very kind never envies, never rude, or self-seeking or keeps a record of what he does for others." He is my protector and I have so much trust in him and so much hope and perseverance. The love that I feel from Jonathan is unconditional. But most of all, I know that his love will forgive me, that is, if I'm pregnant. I will get through this. Olivia said, "Girl that was simply just beautiful." "You are in love with Jonathan and I pray that you're not pregnant. Jonathan sounds like an amazing man. You really can't let him get away. I understand. Let's just make it through this weekend. You will know by Monday.   Lula and Olivia walked back to their dorm rooms. Lula wanted to lie down and take a nap before it was time to meet with Jonathan.

Jonathan walked up to Lula's door and knocked on it. Lula answered the door saying, "hi baby."   Jonathan asked if she would like to get a milk shake something as he stood in the doorway.   Lula said, "Okay,"   let me get my sweater and my purse. Jonathan smiled and they both walked to his truck holding hands. Jonathan went around to open up the door and help Lula inside. They drove away to a local drug store to get a milk shake and not be worried about segregation. Black people were welcome at this drug store. They sat down at a table. There weren't very many tables in the store as it was a small area. There were only four tables and one waiter. He walked over and greeted them saying, "hi" may I help you with something tonight?" Jonathan answered yes please. We would like two milk shakes with strawberries.   Jonathan asked Lula if she would like something else. She answered saying that she wanted some French fries.   Jonathan told the waiter that they also wanted French fries please and handed him the menu.   He grabbed Lula's hand gently and asked her "sweetie how was your day?" She looked into his eyes so intensely talking so softly and quiet saying

"sweetheart my day was good." "I'm glad that it's over and that I
am here with you;" "Oh, I have spoken with Olivia and she would
love to accompany us to the luncheon this Saturday with Booker t.
Washington." I told her about Oscar and she was excited. I also
told Olivia that you and Oscar would pick us up at twelve O'clock
noon. Jonathan said, "I know that Oscar will be very pleased and
good that is confirmed." Jonathan asked Lula what time he
should pick her up for dinner on Sunday. He told her that dinner
would be served at 4:00 PM and that he wanted to be on time, as
he liked to have everything in order and smiled at Lula. Lula said
that she would be ready at 3:00 PM. They continued to have a
good conversation. Jonathan looked at her and said, "You have
something on your lips." He moved his seat closer to her and she
asked if it was off her lips. He moved in closer to her kissing her
on her bottom lip gently sucking on it and saying, "I think that I
got it off." "Yes," whatever it was, it really was good." Lula
started to giggle. They finished their milk shakes and were ready to
leave. Jonathan helped Lula get into the truck and he got in. He
held and kissed her hand that was resting on the seat. He also
pulled her hand close to his heart and she moved closer to him.
He rode down the street with some joy in his heart. She said that
she wasn't ready to go to her room yet and Jonathan asked her
what did she have on her mind. She told him that she just didn't
want to be alone and because she lived on campus, the rules were
clear that no one could stay in the dorm if they didn't live there.
She told him also that she wanted him to hold her. His eyes had
gotten big and he told her that they could get a room at the hotel.
Lula asked if they would have to get a hotel just for him to hold
her. She said, "I don't think so." "We can save that for a
special day. Jonathan agreed with her and asked her if it would
be okay for them to drive over to the River Front. This was an
area where people would go to have picnics as the sun was setting.
Jonathan pulled up in the parking lot and Lula was sitting very
close to him. He asked Lula if she knew what she meant to him.
There was an intense passion that they both felt for each other.
Lula was feeling very comfortable with Jonathan. Out of
nowhere, Lula took off her blouse and Jonathan looked over asking
her if she was sure. Feeling warm with excitement, said, "yes,"

I'm sure.'   He had his eyes on her saying, "Oh my!"   "You look amazing!   She took off her bra and he couldn't believe his eyes.   Not able to speak, he was taken back by her abrupt actions. He asked again, are you sure, we should do this? Lula looked at Jonathan with her eyes so big and bright and said, "Yes this is what I want."   He asked, "May I touch you?" Every time Jonathan would touch Lula's body, he would start to quiver.   He pulled her closer to him as he caressed her body. He began to kiss her breathing real hot and heavy. The windows were all steamed up. Being caught up in their passion in the midst of it all, Jonathan told Lula "God took his time when he created you." He made love to her for about an hour. After an hour, they both got dressed and Jonathan sat and held Lula expressing how he felt about her.   She was very quiet.   Jonathan asked her, "Sweetie, are you alright?"   She said real softly, "yes, I'm fine."   He asked if she was sure.   She said, "Yes Baby, I'm sure."   He asked her if she was ready to go back to her dorm room.   She said, "Yes, we have classes in the morning."   Jonathan agreed telling her that she was right as he started up the truck.   He drove back to the campus. The ride back was very quiet.   Jonathan asked Lula why she was so quiet and wanted to know if she thought that they made the wrong decision.   "No," Lula said.   "I'm happy with you."   "I think that I'm just a little tired."   "I have a lot on my mind as I have a test in the morning for my first class, and I'm wondering if I'm going to do well.   "Please don't think anything else" Jonathan said.   "I'm head over heels for you."   He went around the truck, opened the door, and helped Lula out of the truck.   He also walked her to her room, put his arms around her, hugged and held her tight.   He told her to get some rest and that he would see her in the morning.   As she opened the door and closed it behind her, Jonathan stood there for a while as if he didn't want to leave. Finally, he walked away. Lula stood there in her room putting her purse up and her sweater away.   She started getting ready for bed. All tucked away in bed, she was very deep in thought wondering if she was pregnant, should she tell the professor, what would he do? Would he leave his wife? Maybe he would. She told herself, he did tell me it's not what I think. Maybe this baby would change things.   Lula finally fell asleep.

The next morning, Lula woke up a little late.   She rushed trying to make it to class on time,   running out her door, saying good morning to people that she passed on her way.   Jonathan stood there saying, "Good morning sweetie."   She said, "Hi" I'm sorry, but don't forget I have to make it to class.   I don't want you to think that I'm being rude, but I'm kind of late."   Jonathan took her hand and her books as he ran with her.   They made it to Lula's class just in time.   She turned to Jonathan and kissed him as she left him with a smile.   Her class was two hours long.   She had two more classes for the day.   She also needed to make it to work, had the weekend off, and a very busy weekend.   After class,   Jonathan was waiting for her in the corridor right outside of the cafeteria. He said, "I hope that you don't mind me waiting for you."   "I just wanted you to know that I would like to walk you to your dorm room tonight."   "I would like to make sure that you make it in safely."   Lula said, "Okay,   I get off at 8:00 PM."   He told her "sweetie,   I will see you then" and kissed her before leaving.

Lula went back to the kitchen and started to work preparing tables (cleaning them off),   making salads, and cutting cake.   She continued working for two hours before taking a 25-minute break. During the break, she noticed Olivia waiting for her to find out if their plans for the luncheon were still on for Saturday.   Lula informed her that they would still be attending the luncheon,   it would begin at 1:00 PM,   but that Jonathan would pick them up at 12:00 noon in order to be there on time. Olivia remembered to be ready at 12:00 noon but asked Lula how were they all going to fit in Jonathan's truck.   Lula assured her that they all would be able to ride in the truck.   She encouraged her to just have fun.   Olivia agreed and said,   "Okay, I will make the best of it" and asked Lula how had she been feeling.   Lula told her that she had been good the past few days and Olivia assured her that she would be going to the doctor's appointment with her as she had taken that day off. Lula thanked her and told her that she would have to get back to work and that Jonathan would be there later on that night to walk her back to her dorm room.   Olivia asked how she and Jonathan were doing. Lula looked down, grabbed Olivia's hands,   and let

out a screeching sound. GIRL WEARE FINE! Olivia asked,
"YOU WHAT?" "WHAT ARE YOU DOING?" "BE
CAREFUL, JUST TAKE YOUR TIME." Lula thanked her for her
concern and told her that she would be careful. Olivia let her
know that she didn't mean to pry into her business but that she was
her friend.   Lula assured her that she didn't feel that she was
prying into her business, but that she just didn't love Jonathan, but
it was Henry that she couldn't let go of because he was in her
heart.   Olivia reminded her that Henry was married and that she
didn't see him in her future.   Lula agreed and told her that they
would talk about it later as she had to get back to work. She asked
Olivia to please keep their conversation between the two of them
and she agreed as they were friends and like sisters. Lula
reminded Olivia that she had to get back to work so that she
wouldn't get in trouble for being late and that she would see her
soon. Olivia agreed and they went their separate ways. Lula
went back to work for the next few hours. She finally finished her
tasks and peeked out into the kitchen and saw Jonathan sitting
there waiting for her. She walked toward him and greeted him
with a big hug and a kiss. Jonathan told her that she was so breath
taking. She smiled and kissed him again. He asked her if she
was hungry and she told him no she wasn't hungry, as she had
been nibbling on food at the job.   Jonathan told her that they
needed to talk and asked if they could go somewhere to sit and
talk. Lula said, "Sure, is everything alright?" "Can we just sit
in your truck and talk" "I want to turn in early tonight because we
have the luncheon tomorrow."   Jonathan said, "Yes, I
remember." They walked holding hands moving toward the truck.
Jonathan opened up the door-smiling saying, "after you my love"
Lula continued to smile. Sitting behind the wheel,   Jonathan told
her that he was very sweet on her, the dinner with his parents was
on Sunday, and that he wanted to tell her more about her parents.
His parents were very religious, didn't believe in sex before
marriage, and would feel that his intentions were to marry her as
he was bringing her to dinner.   Jonathan didn't want Lula to be
surprised by his parent's actions.   Lula told him that she
understood and asked if that why he looked so serious. Jonathan
said "yes" as he chuckled to himself.   They talked for another

hour and Jonathan walked her back to her dorm room, as it was time for her to retire for the night.   They hugged and kissed before leaving each other.

Chapter 8 (Saturday Morning)

Lula woke up from a very peaceful sleep. She started preparing
for the day as she went to the bathroom to brush her teeth and wash
her face.   She put a housedress on and went over to Olivia's room
in the same building. She knocked on Olivia's door and she
opened it saying, "I see someone's excited today." Lula asked
her if she was not excited also as she would be meeting Oscar.
Olivia said, "He'd better not be ugly." Lula told her that she was
sure that he wasn't ugly, but it was really just a luncheon. She
explained that she had come over to see what Olivia would be
wearing.   Olivia said that she would be looking good. She asked
Lula if she would be wearing a hat. She said "yes" and Olivia
agreed to wear one too.   Lula left to return to her room to get
ready. She took a bath and got dressed, putting her dress on. It
hung all the way to the floor with a slight tail that followed behind.
The dress buttoned all down her back.   Her hair was pinned up.
She had a matching purse and world pink lipstick. It was now
11:30 AM and she went over to Olivia's room to check on her.
Knocking on the door, she asked if she was ready.   They looked
at each other and laughed because they both had on the same
outfit.   The outfits were white in color.   Their hats were different
colors. Lula's hat was white and Olivia's was silver.   Olivia
told Lula that she looked amazing and Lula complimented her by
saying the same thing.

They could see Jonathan and Oscar from the window. They both
were in suits with vests and had on suspenders. They also had on
very nice shoes all shined up. Their hair was very nicely cut. Both
ladies walked out into the hallway. Jonathan told them both that
they were beautiful and held and kissed Lula's hand. He then
walked over to Oscar and introduced him to Olivia and escorted
him over to her. Oscar did a curtsy and placed Olivia's hand in
his and asked if he could have the pleasure of accompanying her to
the luncheon. He also told Olivia how beautiful she was and she
replied that she would love to attend the luncheon with him.   The

four of them sat very snug in the truck as they went to the local church where the event took place. To make the ride more comfortable, Oscar started to sing in his baritone voice. He sang, "We are Soldiers in the army. We have to fight although we have to cry. We have to hold up the bloodstained banner. We have to hold it up until we die." His song also made the ride more enjoyable. Arriving at the church, the guys helped the ladies down from the truck. Oscar looked very dashing and dapper holding Olivia by her arm very tight and close as if she might get away. She walked with her head held high. Jonathan and Lula followed. They found their reserved table and took their seats at the same table. The men pulled the seats out so that they could sit down. They both sat down by their dates. Olivia smiled, as she was very pleased. There were two other couples at the table also. The other two ladies said "hello" to everyone. The woman sitting across from Oscar recognized him and asked, "Oscar, Oscar, is that you?" He replied, it's me Maggie and the other woman said, "Oh hi, my name is Sarah. Jonathan and Oscar said that they were very pleased to meet both of them. Both of their husbands sat very quietly and said good afternoon and Lula and Olivia smiled. Maggie and Oscar took an algebra class together   Maggie was surprised that Oscar didn't remember her in the beginning.   He finally said, "Oh, okay, yes now I remember you now." Maggie had nothing else to say as her conversation faded away.   Jonathan and Oscar had good conversations with their dates. Everyone enjoyed their dinner.   The announcer mentioned local events being sponsored in the city. Following these announcements, he introduced Booker T. Washington. Mr. Washington walked out and started to mention his 10 accomplishments.   He also stated that he believed that education was the key to success; he knew that women could be educated, but believed that a woman's place was in the home.   He also believed that men should lead and that women should not put themselves in front of their husbands.   Mr. Washington played key roles in both the development of The Tuskegee Institute and in fundraising, securing financial donations for African Americans education. He went on to say that, he was one of the most prominent leaders of African Americans and mentioned one of his most famous speeches that was given on September 18, 1895 and was viewed as one of his most revolutionary moments. He didn't like segregation and didn't fight vocally to support it. He also mentioned being an author and his books revealing his experiences as a slave and his role as advisers to many presidents. His speech continued for a long time, the crowd cheered wild with excitement, and gave him a standing ovation at the end of his speech.   He left as he had another engagement, and members of the audience remained talking. Their conversations went on for an hour after his departure. Oscar asked Olivia if she enjoyed the luncheon. She stated that she really enjoyed herself and that the speaker was amazing;   He walked her out to the parking lot and asked if he could take her out for another date as he really enjoyed her company. She told him yes that she would like that and he took her hand and kissed it. She started to blush.   By this time, Jonathan and Lula walked up to them and Jonathan said, "I see that there is a connection between the two of you." Oscar said, "You did good." "I would like to keep Olivia close." They all got back in the truck and went back to their dorms. Once back at the dorms, Oscar helped both ladies out of the truck. Jonathan greeted Lula as they both walked into the dorm. Not wanting to leave yet, the men stayed and the four of them gathered around conversing, laughing, and singing. Others had come out of their rooms to listen. Oscar had a wonderful voice. That stood out from the others.   It was like a gift from God. Olivia was very happy and smiled from ear to ear.   Everyone enjoyed their company. It was getting late and Jonathan and Oscar had to say their good-byes. Neither one of them wanted to leave, but knew that it was time to go. Standing there with their ladies, Jonathan told Lula that he would be there the next day at 2:00 PM to pick her up and that he loved her. Lula looked into his eyes with her eyes filled with tears. She repeated very slowly, "you love me?" Jonathan held her hand said, "Yes I love you." "I believe that I show you how much I love you." "You know love is not just a word that one says." "It is a true action." "Those four words could mean the world to someone and I hope that we can build a strong foundation that could last a lifetime."   Lula listened very closely with an open heart.   Jonathan walked her to her door and kissed

her good night. Oscar was talking with Olivia, telling her good night as he kissed her on her cheek. He walked away, meeting Jonathan, and they drove away.
Chapter 9 (Sunday Morning)

The next day, Sunday morning, Jonathan was up early as he could only think of Lula. He thought about yesterday and how he poured out his heart to her and that maybe she didn't feel the same way that he felt. Knowing that he was going to meet with her later that day, it weighed heavy on his heart. His heart ached for her. Back at Lula's dorm, it was early and she was feeling restless. She had gotten up to take a walk around campus to clear her head. As she approached the door, she could smell fresh coffee. Yes, it smelled so good. There was a small area off the lobby at the entrance of the front door of the dorm. There was also a lounge area there that contained a coffee pot, a percolator. Lula went to the percolator, poured herself a cup of coffee, and sat down to relax for a moment. Felling the sunshine on her face realizing what she had to face, she felt so surreal. Olivia came in the room and poured herself a cup of coffee. She went over to where Lula was and sat next to her. She held Lula's hand, gave her a hug, and told her that she would be alright. Lula said that she was very scared and Olivia told her that whatever happened, she would be there for her. Lula thanked her and changed the subject. She asked Olivia, "What did you think about Oscar?" Olivia said, "Well, I'm really excited about him girl!" "I wanted to jump his bones but that wouldn't have been lady like." Lula started to giggle. Olivia asked "WHAT? I'm just saying." Lula said, "That's a good thing." "He seems very much into you." She and Olivia talked for the vast part of the morning and finally said that she was going to meet with Jonathan's parents. Olivia asked her how she felt about that. She said on one hand, it was nice and that she knew that Jonathan was very excited about her meeting his parents, but that only Olivia knew about the situation that she was in and that she just couldn't get too excited only to let herself down. "We will have to see what the outcome is" Lula said. Olivia agreed that she was right. Lula told Olivia that she had to leave to get ready. "Okay, I'll see you later, maybe tomorrow" said Olivia.

Lula returned to her room and started to get ready. She did her hair and got dressed. She tried to not over dress or under dress. She wanted to look her best in order for Jonathan's parents to accept her. The time was getting close for Jonathan to pick her up. She was ready and couldn't wait in her room any longer. Feeling very nervous, she walked down to the lounge. She would sit down; get back up looking out of the window. This went on for 15 minutes. Finally, she saw Jonathan pull up. She couldn't wait for him to come in to get her. She walked out of the door. Jonathan saw her, hurried over and said, "hi sweetie." 'You must be really excited, huh?" Lula kissed him and he told her that he liked that. She placed her arms around Jonathan's neck and held on to him tight. He twirled her around placing her back on her feet on solid ground. She grabbed his hand as they skipped to his truck. Jonathan opened the door and helped Lula get inside. He entered the truck from the driver's side. Looking over at Lula, he told her that she was so beautiful. He started the truck up and reached over to hold Lula's hand. He told her to please not be nervous. She was very quiet as she looked over at him and smiled.

Lula and Jonathan were on their way to his parents' house. They lived down a long dirt road on a private piece of property that was given to his grandparents by the slave owners. Jonathan showed Lula their family cemetery where all of his family had been laid to rest and where his parents would be laid to rest. As they pulled up to the house, the two other houses on the private land could be seen. His auntie was in her house and his uncle was in the yard of the other house. They both would usually be at Jonathan's parents' house for Sunday dinner or his parents would be at one of their big houses. They were one big happy family. There wasn't anything that they wouldn't do for each other. There was a big yard where they would have big cookouts and pig roasts for the entire family. Jonathan got out the truck and walked to the other side to open up the door and escort Lula out of the door. Jonathan waved to his auntie as she peeked out of her window her name was Aunt Lorraine. He said "hi" to Uncle Tommy Lee Brooks and told him that he wanted him to meet his girl. Uncle Tommy Lee came over and shook Lula's hand as Jonathan introduced her to him. Jonathan held Lula's hand as they stepped upon the porch and into the house.   "Come on in, Come on in" said Jonathan's father, Joseph. His mother, Janette, was coming from around the kitchen drying her hands. She looked with a big smile on her face and said "hello."   Both of his parents shook Lula's hand and Janette said, "come on in and have a seat." The house was filled with the smell of fried chicken and peach cobbler that was done and cooling off close by the window. Janette said that dinner would be served soon.   As she went to prepare the table, Lula asked if she could help. Miss Janette said, "You may get to know my husband for a minute" and assured her that everything was already done.   The table was set and Miss Janette called for everyone to come to the kitchen.   Jonathan pulled chairs out for Lula and his mother to sit in.   His dad sat at the head of the table and his mother sat at the other end.   Jonathan and Lula sat side by side.   Joseph welcomed Lula to their home and told her not to be nervous, letting her know that they were just good old people who put God first   He also told her that he had been married to his wife for over 25 years and that he loved both her and their children. Jonathan smiled and his mother said, "Okay Joseph, you can open up with a prayer." He said, "Dear heavenly Father, thank you for another day and for the food that you have provided for my family. In Jesus's name, AMEN!"   Everyone else around the table also said "AMEN!"   Jonathan asked his mother if she could please pass the corn on the cob and she said, "Sure baby."   Everyone enjoyed their meal. Following the meal, Jonathan and Lula helped to clear the table. They all sat down again and his mother brought slices of peach cobbler and scoops of vanilla ice cream for everyone.   As they were sitting eating their dessert, Miss Janette asked her son about their plans.   Lula spoke first and told her that she was a student at the same university that her son Jonathan attended.   Miss Janette said that she thought that was nice, but that she did not think that a woman should do any work and that it was a man's job to provide for his wife and family.   Lula said,   "Yes mam.   I understand."   Jonathan asked his mother if he could; please pray that Lula would one day be his wife as that was his intention. Jonathan's dad changed the subject and took his son to the porch. Lula helped Miss Janette clean the table off and helped in the kitchen.

Miss Janette made small talk and made reference to the weather. When all of the cleaning was done, everyone sat on the porch laughing and talking and Joseph telling jokes. He mentioned the funny things that Jonathan did when he was a child. It was getting late and Jonathan and Lula said their good-byes. Lula gave Miss Janette a big hug and thanked her and Joseph for a wonderful time. She and Jonathan got back in the truck and went back to Lula's dorm. Their ride back was a happy one as they sang and laughed. Upon their arrival back to the dorm, they walked inside. Jonathan said, "My parents loved your company and I hope that you feel a little more comfortable." Lula told him that she did feel very comfortable now. Jonathan said, "I will see you in the morning, right?" Lula told him that she had forgotten to tell him that she would be going somewhere with Olivia and that she would see him around six PM on her break. She told him that she had to work Jonathan said, "OH, okay. "I'll see you in the morning," he said looking a little surprised. They both kissed each other good night.

The next morning Lula was up, dressed, and ready to go. She was in the lounge waiting on Olivia. Olivia walked toward Lula saying "good morning." Olivia responded by saying "good morning "to Lula and asked how her visit went with Jonathan's parents. Lula told her that she had a wonderful time, thought that they liked her, the food was good, and that she helped his mother clean the kitchen. Olivia said, "that's great and it seems that you were nervous for no reason and all that you had to do was just be yourself," "Who wouldn't love you?" They both looked out the window for their ride to come. Lula spotted the vehicle and told Olivia that their ride was there. They walked out to the vehicle, got in, paid a local fare. And rode to the hospital. The clinic was adjacent to the hospital, so the driver would know where they wanted to go over on Jefferson Street. The driver asked if she meant South Central Hospital and Olivia said, "yes." Olivia wanted to know if he would wait on them, and he told her that he would. The ladies went inside to the receptionist desk and Lula told her that she had appointment. The receptionist asked for her name and Lula said, "Lula, Lula Hood." The nice lady said, "Let me check." She verified that Lula did have an appointment and handed her some paper work to be completed. Lula completed the paperwork and returned it to the receptionist who told her that the nurse would call her to see the doctor in a few minutes. Olivia and Lula sat patiently waiting for the nurse to call Lula. Fifteen minutes later, the nurse came to the waiting room and called her to come back to the examining room. The nurse walked with her to the examining room and closed the door as they went in. The nurse took her blood pressure, temperature, and weight as she asked Lula to step on the scale. She explained how the test would work. They would take her blood and urine and send the hormone from the blood and inject it into laboratory mice. If the mice reacted in a particular way, that would let them know the outcome. The nurse asked for Lula's last monthly period. She told the nurse that she had missed one period 30 days go. The nurse drew blood from her arm and placed a label on the container with Lula's name on it and told her that the doctor would be in to see her. He was the doctor that Black women in the area saw due to segregation and low income. After Lula waited for 10 minutes, the doctor came in looking over his glasses and said "good morning." "My name is Doctor Daniel Scott and I will be examining you." Lula said "good morning." The doctor also told her that she would need to get undressed and walked out the room. The nurse came back in to give Lula a hospital gown and told her that she needed to take everything off. Lula said "okay." After five minutes, the doctor and the nurse returned back to the room. The nurse explained that Lula that she had to lie back and put her legs up on the stirrups as the doctor needed to check her inside for abnormal tissue and disease. He wanted to make sure that everything was normal. He also checked her breasts and the nurse told her that she would be in the room to assist the doctor. The doctor started the examination explaining every move. Part of this exam was very uncomfortable. The doctor didn't take long. The nurse told Lula that they were done, she could get dressed, and to please make sure that she stopped by the receptionist desk to pay for the visit. Lula got dressed, walked out to the receptionist desk, and paid her $5.00, which was the cost of the visit. She then went over to Olivia (who was waiting for her) and explained what had happened in the doctor's office and how she didn't like the feeling of the pelvic exam. Olivia listened and asked Lula if she was pregnant. Lula said "that she still didn't know and that they would contact her by phone later on in the week."   Lula and Olivia waited outside for their ride.   Once their ride returned, they rode back to the dorm and was just in time for Lula's last class for the day.   She was working hard to make sure that her grades were up to par.   Knowing that she needed to find out her present grade, she checked with her teacher after her last class.   She went to Mrs. Wood's desk and told her that she wanted to know her present grade.   Mrs. Wood said, 'okay, I can check it for you." She checked her record, looked at Lula, and told her that her present grade was a C minus, but that her end of the semester exams hadn't been completed.   She also explained that her final grade would be determined by everything combined. Lula thanked Mrs. Wood and left to go to work.   She had about five minutes to herself before she started her shift.   Knowing that she had only four hours to work tonight, Lula sat down at the table in the cafeteria thinking about the past weekend,   how she was getting to know Jonathan better, but still couldn't get Professor Nixon off her mind.   She also wondered about the pregnancy test and that she could be carrying a baby!   She also thought to herself, well I did sleep with Jonathan and maybe he will think that it's his baby, or maybe I will keep things to myself and not say anything to anyone.   She got up, put her things away on a shelf in the kitchen, and grabbed a clean apron.   She prepared to start her shift.   She would be working hard for the next two hours.   It was break time and Lula walked from the kitchen to the dining area.   There was a table assigned for the employees to sit at while still working.   Jonathan made it to Lula's break on time.   He walked up to Lula and said, "hi sweetie. How was your day?" He leaned over and kissed her. Lula told him that her day was good and asked him about his day. Jonathan told her that his day was good but that he needed to find a job to take care of her.   He didn't like the fact that she had to work those long hours.   Lula said, "Now you know things are changing.   "Women have the right to do a lot of things." "This is the 20th century, I'm getting my education, and I want to be a teacher." "I want better for my children." My mama was born a slave."   ""I know that your mother never had to work and that was great for her, but I want more than just being confined in the house. No disrespect to your mom."   Jonathan said "no disrespect was taken and that he loved her." Lula grabbed his hand and changed the subject.   Jonathan said, "Lula, this is about the third time I have told you how much I love you and I don't hear anything from you." "What is going on?"   Lula said, "I hear you loud and clear." "You are a wonderful man and I do love you." "My love for you is growing stronger each and every day. "It's just that I want to be in love with you."   "When I think about you, I want to think only about you/   Jonathan told her that he would win her heart over all the way, you will see,   Lula said, "okay, I need to get back to work." Jonathan asked if he could walk her to her room when she got off work. "No" Lula said.   "I will be okay." Jonathan told her good night and I will see you in the morning. Lula said, "Okay that will be fine. " "It's not you, I need to get my grades up and I have to work the next two days. "   Jonathan kissed Lula and walked away. Lula went back to work taking care of her responsibilities. Her shift ended at 8:00 PM and she went back to her dorm room, finished her homework, and prepared for the next day.

Lula had to work and go to school for the next few days. Jonathan walked her to her classes and home from work.   It was now Wednesday night and Lula was getting off work. She now had the next two days off from work. Jonathan was there to pick her up and Lula was feeling very relaxed and flirtatious as she held his hand. They went back to Lula's dorm room where Jonathan gave her usual kiss good night. She opened the door and Jonathan was about to walk away when Lula put her finger to her lips making this SSSH sound. She grabbed him by the hand and pulled him inside the door. Jonathan whispered to Lula, what are you doing? You're going to get in trouble. Lula closed the door and leaned against it. She motioned at him with her finger to come to her. Jonathan walked toward her and they kissed each other. He looked at Lula and played with her hair. Overcome with passion, he lifted her up in his arms and carried her over to her bed. They both laid on the bed for a moment and Jonathan told her that she was beautiful and that he couldn't see himself living without her. He slowly kissed her all over her face and told her, I want to make love to you .He kissed her hand and Lula looked at him in a very seductive way. He started to undress her, taking his sweet time unbuttoning her blouse, kissing her shoulder. He also took off her skirt, slowly kissing her stomach, then her thighs, gently removing her stockings. He rubbed her feet, kissed her toes looked, at her body and paused for a moment admiring the smooth touch of her skin. He kissed every inch of her body, not missing a spot. Lula was feeling very light without a care in the world. It was like she left all of her problems on the other side of the door. Jonathan made love to Lula and their bodies intertwined in passion trying not to make a lot of noise. The passion just couldn't be contained. Lula enjoyed each and every moment. Jonathan held her so tight as both of their bodies poured of sweat. He was so caught up in making love to Lula that he began to cry. He said out loud through tears running down his face "you don't know how much I love you." "I have never felt this way about any woman." He also screamed out loud "Lula! " "Lula!" Receiving the impact of Jonathan's love, neither one of them got any rest that night. Finally, they both fell asleep in each other's arms. Jonathan woke up as he laid there stroking her hair, giving her soft kisses. Lula woke up as Jonathan gazed at her. She gave him a big smile and asked what time was it. He told her that it was 3 AM. She grabbed for him and went back to sleep. They both felt good and he could hear her panting in his arms.

At 6 Am Lula woke up in Jonathan's arms. She whispered to him very softly, calling his name, you must get dressed and leave before I get myself in trouble. He got dressed and kissed her good - bye . He told her that he would see her later on. Lula smiled. He looked out the door and made it to his truck before anyone could suspect him of leaving. Later on that morning, Lula prepared for the day before walking out of the dorm. The phone rang as she was half way down the stairs She went back to answer it saying, "Hello."   The other party on the phone was from the clinic.   The woman said "hello" and asked if she was Lula Hood. She said, "Yes this is Lula."   The woman said, "We have results of your pregnancy test."   "Yes, you are having a baby! "   Lula asked, "Are you sure?"   The woman said "yes!   I am very sure, now you have a very nice day."   Lula told her okay thank you. She sat down with a very stunned look on her face.   She sat there for a moment trying to get herself together. Leaving her room, walking down the stairs, on her way to class, Lula looked over and saw Olivia. Olivia asked her what was wrong.   She said very quietly, "That was the clinic."   As she talked, her eyes got really big and she began to cry.   "They said that I'm pregnant," said Lula.   Olivia sat beside her and gave her a tight hug and told her that she was going to be alright.   Lula kept on crying and Olivia sat with her for another 15 minutes.   She helped Lula get herself together.   They both knew that they had to make it to class on time.   Olivia said, "I'll see you later, okay?"   Lula said, "Okay, I don't have to work tonight or the next day."   She made it through the day,   had a hard time concentrating, but made it successfully and the day was done.   She walked out of class and Jonathan was waiting for her. They hugged each other and Jonathan asked her how her day went.   "It was very busy" Lula said and asked Jonathan how his day was. "It was very good and now even better since I'm with you," Jonathan said.   Lula smiled and Jonathan asked about her plans for the night. She told him that she had made plans to meet with Olivia and that they were going to study and listen to some music on the radio, but that she hoped to see him around 8 o'clock PM.   Jonathan smiled at her and they walked back to her dorm room and kissed until later.

Lula had been back at the dorm for about 5 minutes when Olivia knocked on the door.   Olivia let herself in and she asked how her day went and how was she feeling. I "I'm a little nervous and scared."   "I really thought that the clinic was going to tell me that I wasn't pregnant."   "I don't know what I'm going to do" Lula said.   Olivia told her not to do anything until she started to show and that no one had to know.   She also told her that she thought that she and Jonathan could make a life for themselves. She also encouraged her to tell Jonathan that the baby was his and that she had heard the two of them the night before making out. She said, "I wasn't trying to listen, but he was crying or something." "I know one thing, Jonathan is in love with you, and you need to be falling his way." "I won't lie to Jonathan and I know that he won't ask me though." "I will try to keep this to myself as long as I can."   "Thank you Olivia for always having me as your sister," Lula said.   They both talked for the next few hours. It was getting later and Olivia knew that Jonathan would be coming. She told Lula that she would talk to her later on tomorrow. Lula said "okay" and closed the door. She had a little time by herself contemplating and talking to God.   She asked God to make things right, give her directions and to help her to do the right thing. She said, "God please help me." "I'm scared. "Give me a sign or something just to let me know that you really can hear me God!" There was a strong knock at the door. KNOCK! KNOCK! KNOCK! Lula went to the door and Jonathan stood there saying, "hi sweetie." She almost jumped in his arms. He asked her if she was okay. As he held her so tight. They both sat on the bed and Lula held on to Jonathan. She didn't want to let him go. He asked her what was wrong and she said, "I have just had a very long week and I want to thank you for being in my life"   Jonathan pulled Lula's hair out of her eyes, looked her in her face, and said, "I love you." "I love you so very much." Lula told him that she loved him too and hugged him a little tighter.   Jonathan held her until she fell asleep. He kissed and held her all night.

Lula had to work eight-hour shifts on Saturday and Sunday that weekend. She worked normal days feeling like something was different. She felt optimistic. One of her tasks included bringing coffee cups from the kitchen to set the table. As she looked across the room carrying the cups, she almost dropped them as she saw Professor Henry Nixon. Her heart skipped a beat and she tried to hold herself together. She also tried to ignore him. The professor sat by himself. It looked like he was waiting on his other colleagues.   Lula fought the thought of going over to confront

him. Her hand began to get nervous. Rubbing her hands together, she began to walk his way. She told Professor Nixon good morning. I need to talk to you. He told her to please have a seat and that he had a few minutes.   Lula told him that she wouldn't keep him a very long time and would get straight to the point. She said, "I'm pregnant." The professor said "congratulations." "I know that the father must be very happy." Lula said, "You know that you are the father of this child." He said, "I don't know what you're talking about." She felt very distraught and told him that she just thought that he would want to know." "I didn't know that you were such an asshole," Lula said. She got up, walked away, and went back to work. She finished the rest of her tasks, had a lot on her mind, and was very tired by the end of her workday.   Jonathan was standing waiting for Lula. He had flowers for her. She knew now that her future was with Jonathan. She also felt that he would be someone that she could count on.   Jonathan said "hi sweetie" and Lula greeted him with a kiss.   He told her that he had come to escort her home and that he had brought her some flowers.   He said, "They are beautiful but not as beautiful as you are. "I have something special for you" Lula looked at him, smiled, and asked, "what is my surprise? He told her sweetheart you can trust me, I will walk you to my truck, but when you get in, I will have to blindfold you, okay. Lula said, 'okay with a big smile on her face." Jonathan walked her to his truck and told her that it was time to put the blind fold on. She said okay. He placed the blind fold on Lula and talked to her at the same time.   He said, "Don't cheat." He also asked her if she could see and she said, "No, I can't see anything." He told "okay.'   Lula asked, "What is it?"   Jonathan said, "just be patient as he pulled off and drove to their destination.
"   Arriving to the surprise,   Jonathan said with so much joy and excitement, "we are here.   Let me help you out of the truck first before I take your blindfold off. Just give me a minute." He went around the truck to help her down and her over to where he started to take off her blindfold. Lula opened her eyes, smiled, and jumped for joy, saying, "no one has ever done something this special for me."   She looked at the picnic in the park; Jonathan helped her sit down on a blanket.   He had a basket of food and

goodies that his mother had prepared for him.   He started to feed
Lula and kissed her.   Lula smiled and they both shared a very
romantic evening talking, singing, and relaxing in each other's
arms.   Jonathan took Lula's shoes off and rubbed her feet.   Lula
forgot all of her problems as she was so wrapped up in Jonathan.
She wished that she had never met Professor Henry Nixon.   The
day was ending and it started to get dark outside.   Lula and
Jonathan watched the sun set.   Jonathan said that it was time for
him to get Lula to her room.   She agreed and they packed up
their things from the picnic.   They went to the truck and drove
back to Lula's dorm room.   She moved very close to Jonathan and
thanked him for loving her.   He told her, I love you with all of me
and at this point, I really don't think I could love another woman
the way that I love you.   Lula told him that she loved him too.
Back at the room,   Jonathan went in and they shared their night
together. It was a very passionate night and Lula danced,
performed, and entertained Jonathan showing him how much she
loved him.   Their passion was so deep and they both enjoyed each
and every moment.   They fell asleep in each other's arms wishing
that this night would never end.

Chapter 10

For the next two months, Lula and Jonathan made it through the
semester. They passed their classes and were head over heels in
love with each other. Jonathan's parents had invited them to a pig
roast. The whole family would be there. This was July and they
were celebrating the United States of America. This wasn't
known as a legal holiday like Christmas. Independence Day has
been celebrated as far back as 1791. It was only made to be a
legal holiday in 1941. Jonathan and Lula arrived at Jonathan's
parents' house.   It was a beautiful, bright, sunny and hot day.
The temperature was well over 90 degrees. They both got out of
the truck and Jonathan helped Lula to get down.   They walked
arm in arm.   They saw the pig in the roaster outside in the yard.
Jonathan's dad, Joseph and his uncle Tommie Lee cooked all of
the meat. There were a host of other relatives there. Joseph was
so happy to see them both. He said, "hi son!" "Hi Ms. Lula.
"How y'all doing?"   "It's really good to see you both." He
asked Lula "what are you doing to my son?" "He's looking
mighty happy."   Uncle Tommie Lee said, "Hello" you know
what he's doing." "You've been his age before"   Joseph said to
Lula, "Mama is in the kitchen with Jonathan's auntie." "Go on
in the house and say hello."   Lula and Jonathan went inside to
where his mama was sitting at the kitchen table with Jonathan's
aunts Nig and Mattie B. Holding Lula close to him, Jonathan
said "hello mama, Aunt Nig, and Aunt Mattie B."   He kissed
them all. His mama was excited about them coming and said
"Look at y'all." "Somebody is also glowing."   She also said
"what did I tell y'all Nig and Mattie B?" "I have been dreaming
about fish."   Jonathan asked, "What does that mean mama?"   "It
means that someone is pregnant," his mama said. He said, "Well I
don't know who that could be"   Jonathan said.   Lula didn't say a
word. She had put on a few pounds and she did have a glow on
her face. Jonathan told everyone that he was going back outside
with his daddy and uncles. He left Lula in the kitchen with the
ladies. No one said anything for a few minutes. Jonathan's
mother, Mrs. Jeanette asked Lula, "How long are you going to

keep it from my son that he's going to be a daddy?" Lula was drinking some water and listening to Jonathan's mom when the water went down the wrong pipe choking her because of what was just said to her. She got herself together before she decided to answer Jonathan's mom. She said, "Well I'm not sure." "I'm not sure that I'm pregnant." "I have a doctor's appointment." Mrs. Jeanette said, "You don't need a doctor to see that you are with child." "Anyone can see that." "Only my son can't see what's going on." Lula didn't say much as she helped them out and kept to herself. Jonathan's mom and auntie were shucking corn and holding some very interesting conversations about church and other things, including Jonathan. Family was everywhere enjoying each other's company. Everyone was outside in the big yard where 3 families shared the yard. Out of nowhere, Jonathan said very loudly, "Can I have everyone's attention?" He walked over to Lula, got down on one knee, took her hand. He took out a box, opened it up. There was a ring inside of it. He took the ring out, looked up at Lula and asked her "will you do me the honor of being my wife?" Lula was taken by surprise. She grabbed Jonathan by the neck and Said, "YES!" 'yes1" 'YES!" She cried tears of joy. Jonathan's parents made their way to both of them and celebrated the great news. The family made speech after speech welcoming Lula to the Brooks family. The food was ready for them to eat. Everything was delicious. There was cake, watermelon, peach cobbler, ice cream, roasted pig, ribs, rib tips, chicken, smoked salmon, corn on the cob, greens, corn bread, etc. They also drank moonshine, mostly the adult men. Everyone had good family fun dancing and singing. They had a family talent show singing their favorite songs, entertaining each other. It started getting dark and the insects were biting. The men of the family started a fire pit. Everyone watched the men as they lit the fireworks. All of the family gathered together sitting close to their loved ones. Jonathan sat with Lula watching the fireworks. He held her tight, kissing her down her face. He also whispered in her ear how much he loved her. They both shared the rest of the night with Jonathan's parents as it was getting late and they would have to travel a distance to get back to their dorms.   Mrs. Jeanette had asked the two of them to stay the night. They both said, "Yes and that they would feel more comfortable going home in the morning. Mrs. Jeanette made the bed for Lula. She made sure that her stay was comfortable. Jonathan had to sleep on the couch because the two of them were not married. Lula lay in the bed thinking how happy she had been this day and how much she enjoyed the celebration. Jonathan sneaked in the room where Lula was making sure that she was okay. He asked her, "Sweetie are you okay?" She said, "Yes now go and get on the sofa." "Wait" she said as she went to the door. Putting her arms around Jonathan, she said, "I love you." He said, "I love you too. Out of respect, they slept in separate areas of his parents' house. They got a good night sleep.

They woke up the next morning to the smell of fresh coffee, bacon, homemade biscuits and homemade jam.   Mama Jeanette was in the kitchen making breakfast for her family. After Jonathan and Lula washed their faces and brushed their teeth, they walked in the kitchen. Jonathan said "good morning mama"   and Lula said "good morning Mrs. Jeanette. Mrs... Jeanette told Lula that she didn't have to call her Mrs. Jeanette but could call her mama. Lula said, "Okay mama." Jonathan looked at both of them and smiled.   He said, "They were the two most beautiful women in the world."   He then went outside where his dad and uncle were and let them know breakfast was ready. He told them to go on in and eat.   His father said, "Son I'm really happy that you're getting married, but make sure that you love her." "Son what I'm trying to say is, you don't just marry someone because they are pregnant." "Because if that's the reason, well son, it's not going to work." "Marry her because you really truly can love her. Jonathan looked at his dad and said "dad I love this woman with everything that I have in me." "I want to spend the rest of my life with Lula. and oh by the way, I think that I would know if my girl was pregnant."   Dad looked at Uncle Tommy Lee and they both started to laugh. Uncle Tommy Lee changed the subject saying "Jonathan when are we going to go fishing again?"   Jonathan said "anytime unc, anytime."   Everyone was now at the kitchen table eating and having good conversation. Jonathan looked at Lula and asked himself how did he not know that his woman pregnant. Looking at Lula, he could see yes, there was a glow about her. He then said, "Sweetheart are you feeling okay?" She looked at Jonathan, smiled, and said, "Yes, yes, I'm fine." An hour had passed and Jonathan and Lula helped mama clean the kitchen placing everything in its place. All done, it was time to get back to the dorm. They said their good - byes to everyone. Back in the truck, Jonathan and Lula were on their way back to the dorm. Jonathan asked Lula "I'm not saying that you are, but is there a chance that you could be pregnant with my child? She was very quiet and took a moment before answering him. Lula said, "I'm not sure." "I have to make an appointment to find out." Johnathan said, "I want to go to the doctor when you make the appointment." "I don't want to miss a thing." "I can't believe it; I'm going to be a dad!" As they kept riding, Lula just stayed quiet and smiled. They arrived back to the dorm and Jonathan walked Lula to her room. He went in and put his arms around her saying "sweetie everything will be okay and that he would see her later on tomorrow." He also told her that he needed to go and check on a job that he had applied for. Lula said, "Good night and I'll see you soon." Jonathan left.

Lula got ready to relax. She took a nice hot bath, put on her pajamas, and listened to the radio. There was a soft knock at the door. She opened the door. It was Olivia. Lula said, "Hi come on in." She came in and asked her about her visit with Jonathan's parents. Lula said, "Well, it was good and not so good." Olivia asked, "What do you mean?" Lula put her hand out to show Olivia that she was engaged to be married. Olivia said, "That is great." "I am truly happy for you!" Lula said there is much more! Olivia said, "What?" "This is great news." Lula said, Jonathan thinks that I may be pregnant." "He wants to go to the doctor when I go to find out!" Olivia said, "Well when you get ready to go back to the doctor, just tell him that he can't go back in the examination room and has to wait in the waiting room." Lula told Olivia, "Okay, I will." They talked and listened to the radio. Lula showed off her ring and Olivia asked, "When is the wedding?" Lula said, "I'm not sure. We haven't made any plans yet." Olivia asked Lula to keep her informed and let her know when her plans were completed. She left Lula's dorm room and they both retired for the night.

The next morning Jonathan arrived at Lula's room around 11:30 AM. He was very excited as he knocked at the door. Lula opened the door and Jonathan said, "Sweetie I have a job. I will still be able to go to school. I'm not going to give up on my education." Lula told him that was great and asked him when would he start the job. Jonathan said that he would start working the next day. Lula was quiet and Jonathan asked if anything was wrong and that he thought that she would be happy for him. Lula said, "I'm happy, it's just that I had made that doctor appointment to see if I'm pregnant." Jonathan told her that he couldn't make that appointment, but promised that he would be at the next one and would drop her off. Lula said that the appointment would be at the clinic over by the hospital. Jonathan said, "Okay sweetie. I wish that I could be there with you. I think that it's very important and that's why I've started to work so we can get our own place. If we are having a baby, I can't have my wife out here working." Lula told Jonathan that he was right and that if they were pregnant, she would schedule her doctor visits around his work schedule. She emphasized, "If I'm pregnant and we will have to wait and see." Jonathan suggested that they get something to eat. Lula agreed since that would be his last free day before starting to work. She grabbed her purse and said, "I know that you're going to be too busy for me." Jonathan let her know that he would never allow anything or anyone except God come before her. He grabbed her around her waist, rubbed her stomach, and told her that she had gained a few pounds that he called love pounds. "That's not funny," Lula said. Jonathan looked into her eyes seriously and told her that they would be married soon. He also let her know that he fell in love with her and her beauty the first day that he saw her and that she was simply stunning. He suggested again that they go to get something to eat. Lula smiled as they walked down the stairs leaving the dorm headed for the truck.   Jonathan said, "I have an idea." "There's a baseball game at the park.   What do you think about going?" Lula told him that sounded like a lot of fun and Jonathan mentioned that it would be a nice trip driving to the park in Alabama.   The game would be played by the Black Negro League an independent team formed back in the early 1900's.   The name of the team was the Birmingham Giants.   Other teams also played in Alabama.   There weren't any local teams in Mississippi, so Jonathan loved following the closest teams in his area.   In the early 1900's, black men couldn't play baseball with the white teams.   This was another form of segregation and sadly as black people, we could only enjoy only watching our teams.   Some of these Negro baseball teams would travel all over the United States to play other Negro teams.   They finally made it to the game and it was intense.   The Birmingham Giants were up to bat.   The bases were loaded.   The player was up with his bat in his hand. The pitcher threw the first ball and the umpire said, "Strike one." The pitcher threw another ball and the umpire said, "Strike two." The third ball was thrown by the pitcher and the ball was hit out of the park.   Jonathan was excited enjoying the game.   Lula enjoyed her time with Jonathan sitting and eating the goodies that were sold at the concession stands. They laughed and just enjoyed each other.   When the game was over, it was time for them to head back to Mississippi. They enjoyed good conversation during the drive back as they planned their wedding.   Jonathan asked Lula if she would consider getting married in September as they both were still going to school and working.   They would also have to consider the baby. Lula said, "that would be wonderful and I can't wait to be your wife"   The ride was long and Jonathan knew that he had to get back so that he could get some rest and be prepared for work.   They finally made it back to Mississippi to Lula's dorm.   Jonathan got out and helped her out of the truck and walked her to her room. He said "good night and kissed her before he left."   He also told her before I forget; I will be here to pick you up around 7:30 AM.   I have to get to the new job in the morning and I love you. Lula said, "Okay."   I love you too>" Jonathan left.

The next morning Lula was up, ready, and waiting for Jonathan to pick her up for her doctor's appointment at the clinic. She looked out the window and saw Jonathan pulling up. She rushed out to the truck so that he wouldn't have to help her get in. She didn't want to make him late getting to the job on his first day. She jumped into the tuck and said "good morning!" Jonathan said "good morning sweetie." They both were very happy listening to songs on the radio and holding each other's hand. Jonathan told Lula that his dad would pick her up, as he didn't want her to worry about how she would get home. They arrived at the clinic and Johnathan got out, walked her inside, and told her to let him know as soon as she found out something. Lula stopped him and told him that he was more nervous than she was, they would have to run tests, and that she was sure that it would be a few days before they knew anything. Jonathan kissed her good - bye and said that he would see her later on that evening. Lula said, "Okay, have a good day at work." When Lula was done with her doctor's appointment, she went to the front of the lobby to wait on her soon to be father-in-law. She could see Mr. Brooks getting out of the truck waving at her. He helped her into the vehicle and asked her "how are you?" She said, "I'm fine" and thanked him for coming to pick her up as she really appreciated him." Arriving back at the dorm, Mr. Joseph asked Lula "well what did the doctor say about your pregnancy?" "Am I going to be a grandfather? She said very slow, "we will have to wait and see." She was having a hard time getting out of the truck It was clear that she was pregnant Mr. Joseph escorted her to the door and said, "Okay dear. I will see you soon." "Please keep me and my wife informed as to what is going on." Lula told him that as soon as the test came back, she would let them know. As she walked back to her dorm room, she saw Olivia who said, "Hello how have you been and where are you coming from?" Lula replied that Jonathan had taken her to the clinic to see if she was pregnant. Olivia said, "Oh, okay! "I got you!" "I understand!" "I feel that you're doing the right thing..." "I feel that you're doing the right thing. "He doesn't have to know that his is not the father of your baby!" She changed the subject telling Lula that her Uncle Willie and Aunt Seal wanted them to come to a special program at their church on Sunday August 26, 1906 at Good Hope Baptist Church in Vicksburg Mississippi.   She went on to explain that Aunt Seal felt like Lula was a daughter to her and that she wanted to make sure that she could come.   Lula told her that yes she would be there.   Olivia asked her to let her know the results of her letting Jonathan know that she was pregnant.   Lula said, "Okay, I will."

Later on that day, Jonathan went to Lula's dorm room and told her about his hard day at work.   He mentioned that he had worked in a garage cleaning up and taking parts out of vehicles.   He was not a licensed mechanic, but could get his license being trained on the job.   This wasn't what Jonathan wanted to do the rest of his life. Having only a year of college under his belt,   this job would do for the present time.   He could one day reach his goal.   Lula told him that she had cooked him a meal of fried chicken, mashed potatoes, green beans with ham hocks, homemade biscuits, and sweet ice tea.   Jonathan was very pleased with the meal.   After completing the meal, Jonathan asked her what did the doctor say. She said,   "He said that I looked pregnant."   "I have all of the symptoms, but we have to just wait on the test to be sure." Jonathan said, "I can't wait to find out."   "I want to love my baby and my wife."   He told her also,   speaking of you being my wife; I know that we made plans for us to get married in September. How would you feel about getting married at my parents' house? The place is really perfect and we can do it there.   We can have a big garden wedding.   Lula agreed with him saying,   "It sounds really beautiful."   She smiled at Jonathan and he asked her about her plans for the next day.   Lula told him that she needed to enroll for her classes for the fall and that she would need a sitter for the baby. She asked Jonathan if he thought that his mother could watch their child.   Jonathan looked at Lula and said, "you already know that you're pregnant, don't you?"   "I'm just trying to prepare for the worst."   "Oh, before I forget, Olivia was by and asked me to go to Vicksburg next month."   "They are having a special program for her auntie and uncle and I'm going to try and make it."   He suggested that maybe he and Oscar could hang out, go fishing, or something. Lula thought that that was a great idea and wondered if Olivia would stand up for them when they got married.   Jonathan liked that idea and mentioned asking Oscar to be his best man.   They talked the rest of the night and enjoyed each other.   They finally fell to sleep in each other's arms.   His hand was on her stomach.   They both were awakened by the movement in her stomach.   Yes, it was the baby's first time moving.   Jonathan said, "I don't need a doctor to tell me that you're pregnant."   He held her tighter.   They went back to sleep.

Jonathan woke up early the next morning at 6:00AM, as he knew that he had to go to work.   He kissed Lula and her stomach before leaving the dorm room. The next few days were just like the last ones.   Jonathan continued picking Lula up and going to work. This day was a little different.   Lula greeted Jonathan with the news of her being officially pregnant and said hi.   He looked at Lula and asked what was wrong. She said, "We are having a baby."   Jonathan was so full of joy.   He picked Lula up and twirled her around. "Yes we are," he said.   They went to dinner and continued to make wedding plans afterwards.   They also called Jonathan's parents. His mother answered the phone by saying "hello."   Jonathan said "mama?"   Jeanette said, "Yes baby! Jonathan told her, you're going to be a grandma!   His mom was quiet for about a minute and then said, "CONGRATULATIONS!"   They could hear his parents in the background sharing in on the joy and excitement.   Jonathan and Lula ended their conversation with Jonathan's parents and he took Lula's hand and began dancing around the room to their own music. Jonathan sang to Lula, stopped, got on his knees, and put his ear to her stomach. He listened first and then began kissing her stomach saying, "I love you so much and you know that you make my heart skip a beat at just the mention of your name."   He kissed Lula and told her, you know we will be married in a few months. He continued kissing her and slowly began undressing her while taking down her hair. He smelled her hair, he said, "Your hair is so beautiful."   Jonathan put her face in both of his hands and slowly kissed her lips, nibbling on her ears and tasting her sweet kisses. He also undressed, taking off his shirt first, and then removing his pants. Standing together nude, Jonathan led Lula to the bathroom. He guided her to the tub where he had bath water waiting.   Lula stepped in first, then Jonathan following her, lathered up the bath towel with peppermint soap. He washed her body all over and she washed his. They both played being silly and having fun in the bathtub. Jonathan picked her up out of the tub, carried her to the bed.   Drying her body off, he poured nice soothing hot oil on her body, massaging her temples and slowly rubbing and massaging her shoulders, then her back and buttocks. He enjoyed each part of her body.   He also massaged her thighs, rubbed her feet, and she was completely mesmerized.   Lying on his back, Jonathan felt so close to Lula.   She climbed on the bed as she laid her head on his chest. Lula said, "Listen." Jonathan asked what is it. She 'answered our hearts beat as one. They enjoyed soft kisses and good conversation, making plans for their life. Jonathan held Lula into the wee hours of the night.   Knowing that he had to go to work in the morning, he fell asleep. They continued these activities for the next four or five weeks.   July had come and gone.

Chapter 11

Now it was August,   and Lula was really pregnant and showing.
This was the weekend to go to Vicksburg for the special event for
her Auntie Seal.   She and Olivia had purchased their tickets and
they were on their way.   As Lula stepped off the train, the
conductor held her hand.   The first person that Lula saw was
Auntie Seal.   Olivia was right behind her.   Aunt Seal said,   "Oh
my! It looks like you're going to have a baby."   "I'm so happy
for you!"   Olivia and Lula greeted Auntie Seal saying,   "Hello"
and they hugged and kissed each other.   Olivia and Lula got their
luggage and walked to the truck where Uncle Willie Earl was
waiting for them in the train station's parking lot.   He was so
happy to see them.   He never mentioned the fact that Lula was
pregnant.   Everyone got seated in the truck and they started to
Aunt Seal and Uncle Willie Earl's place.   Olivia and Lula's
conversations were about school and how they were ready for the
fall semester.   Aunt Seal told them how proud she was of them
and that there weren't many women that wanted to be educated.
She also emphasized the fact that they were colored women who
were determined to be educated.   Uncle Willie agreed with her.
They arrived to the house and Aunt Seal began to set the dinner
table.   She had prepared pork chops, sweet peas, candied yams,
and homemade apple pie.   The dinner was wonderful and Olivia
and Lula helped her clean the kitchen after the meal.   They all sat
on the porch for a while enjoying the night air.   The weather was
very hot as the temperature was well into 90 degrees.   Finally, it
was time to go to bed.   The ladies said "good night" to Aunt Seal
and Uncle Willie Earl and everyone retired, as they wanted to be
on time for church the next morning.   Everyone was asleep except
Lula.   It was so quiet you could hear the crickets chirping.   She
was wide awake looking at the ceiling thinking about her life and
the things that had happened this past year,   that she was getting
ready to marry Jonathan, and how much she had grown to love
him.   In her mind, she also still had feelings for the professor
Nixon.   She asked herself how could she could still have feelings
for such a heartless man.   But it was true; she had a special place

in her heart that she was saving for the professor.   Finally, she fell
asleep.

Everyone was up early the next morning getting ready for church.
They put on their Sunday best and loaded up in the truck.   It was a
very hot morning as it was still 90 degrees.   Uncle Willie drove
and they finally made it to Good Hope Baptist Church.   Once
inside, they approached the other members and Aunt Seal was
very happy to show off her girls.   She introduced them to her
friends.   Some of the people were still outside but began to
congregate and walk inside.   Everyone was seated and the pastor
wasn't in the pulpit.   The deacons prepared for devotion.   They
read from the bible.   There were three separate devotions.   One
of the deacons started singing the song "He's Sweet I Know."
The congregation sang along.   The pastor walked up to the pulpit
and said "good morning church."   The congregation responded
back saying "good morning."   The pastor said, "I want to thank
the Lord for this opportunity to come before you this morning."
"Now, I want everyone to turn to your neighbor and say neighbor
I'm glad for another day!"   Everyone greeted each other and went
back to their seats.   The pastor began to speak saying, "for those
of you who may not know me,   my name is Rev. Hill."   "We
will now hear the morning announcements and will have a song
from the choir following the announcements.   How about that?"
The choir sang and everyone was into the song as they sang and
clapped.   Following the song there was a special service for some
of the members who had gone beyond the call of duty.   They
called Aunt Seal up for an award.   Lula and Olivia stood up and
clapped so proudly.   Pastor Hill gave a few more comments
before he preached his Sunday Service. He preached a long
sermon.   Some of the members had gotten happy and
experienced the Holy Ghost and shouted.   The pastor opened the
doors of the church when his sermon was completed.   He then
dismissed church for the day.   Everyone didn't leave yet as dinner
would be served in the kitchen for those who wanted to stay. Lula
walked outside and Olivia was close behind her.   Before she
made it to the front door,   a big splash of water came rushing

down her legs. It scared Lula so bad and she turned to Olivia and told her "I'm in trouble."   Olivia asked her what was wrong. Lula showed her the water on the floor and Olivia ran immediately to find Aunt Seal and asked her to hurry to evaluate what was happening with Lula.   Aunt Seal sat Lula down in a chair. Her clothes were soaked and she told Aunt Seal that she felt a little funny.   Aunt Seal told her that she would get one of the church members who would know what to do.   She went to get Martha Newton as she was a mid-wife. Her husband, Frank Newton, went to the kitchen where his wife Martha was, stood close by her, and pointed her out to Aunt Seal.   She and Aunt Seal went to Lula.   Martha asked Lula how far along she was with the pregnancy.   Lula told her that she wasn't sure. Martha also asked her if she was in any pain.   Lula said, "No I'm not in any pain."   Martha told her that she would be in pain soon that it didn't look like she was even close to full term, and that she would need to go to bed so that she could get as comfortable as she could. She also told her that she wasn't sure that her baby would survive, as she would give birth soon.   She got her up, walked her to the truck, and asked that Olivia and Aunt Seal follow her and her husband to their house.   She explained to Lula that she had delivered a lot of babies and that she would charge her $5.00. Lula said, "Yes mam". "I understand."   Everyone was excited and scared as they walked slowly to Martha and Frank Newton's truck.   Aunt Seal and Uncle Willie Earl followed close behind Martha and Frank Newton.   They arrived at the Newton's home and got out assisting them with helping Lula inside. Martha told everyone that it was going to be a long night, as she didn't believe Lula would deliver the bay anytime soon because she wasn't in any pain.   She told them that she would get word to everyone when she would go into labor. She also explained that she had to keep her on bed rest to keep her from getting any kind of infection, that they would have to make her a slop jar, and that she would be fine. Olivia told Martha that she wanted to stay with Lula and she agreed.   Martha walked Aunt Seal and Uncle Willie Earl to their truck, told them that everything would be alright, and that she would call them if anything changed. Aunt Seal said, "Please let me know and I will be back in a heartbeat."   Ms.   Martha

waved good - bye as they left.   She walked back into the house
and checked on Lula as she was lying in bed resting.   She sat by
her side and asked Olivia if she could offer her something to drink.
Olivia said that she would love something to drink.   Ms.   Martha
checked with Lula to see how she was feeling.   She helped her to
get out of her wet clothes and gave her a sponge bath and a gown
to wear.   Lula couldn't have anything to eat for fear that it would
make her sick.   If she went into labor soon, it could cause her to
choke.   Ms.   Martha told Lula that she could have a sip of water
for now.   Olivia kept Lula comfortable.   She rested very
comfortably the rest of the day and night. Ms.   Martha checked
on her throughout the night to see if she in any pain or discomfort.

The next morning was the same as Lula wasn't in any pain.   She
started asking if she could have something to eat.   Ms.   Martha
told her that she could have a few crackers and some soup to keep
her nourished.   She brought her some homemade chicken noodle
soup.   Olivia had a big bowl of soup also.   Lula made it into the
morning without any pain. Ms.   Martha was getting concerned
and let Lula know that if she didn't go into labor soon,   she would
have to take her to the closest hospital in Jackson Mississippi.
Lula said that she understood.   Olivia sat there very quietly and
finally asked Lula if she wanted her to call Jonathan.   Lula said,
"no, not yet." Olivia tried to keep Lula entertained.   Then out of
nowhere, Lula started to have cramps in her back.   Ten minutes
later, it happened again.   The pains started getting worst.   This
went on for the rest of the night. Lula had been in labor for 48
hours.   Ms. Martha checked her cervix to see if the baby was in
the birth canal. Ms.   Martha said that yes finally she could see the
baby's little head.   Lula was in so much pain yelling out loud.
Olivia was wiping her forehead and holding her hand.   She and
Ms.   Martha also held Lula's legs.   The baby's head was poked
out, next the shoulders, and then Ms.   Martha could see the full
body.   "It's a boy," she said.   She started cleaning out the
baby's mouth and cut the umbilical cord.   Lula gave a sigh of
relief thinking that she was done. Ms.   Martha told her that she
had one more push.   Olivia asked her what is that?   Ms.

Martha told her that Lula would have push out the placenta.   The
baby boy was all cleaned up and Ms. Martha smacked the baby
on his behind to make sure that he was alive.   The baby cried and
that was a good sign.   She handed the baby to Lula and asked
Lula for a name for him.   She told Ms.   Lula that she wanted to
name him McKinley after her brother.   Olivia said, "That's a
very proud name."   "I like the name and this baby look just like
Professor Nixon."   Lula was holding him and admiring her
newborn baby. Not long afterwards, Ms. Martha brought in
paperwork for her to complete on the acknowledgement of her
child. She told her that by law she was required to keep a record
of all of the births of children that she delivered in the area.   Lula
said that she understood.   Ms. Martha called Aunt Seal to let her
know that the baby had been born.   Olivia said that she would be
going back to Aunt Seal's house.   Ms. Martha recommended
that Lula and the baby stay with her for the next few days.   Aunt
Seal and Uncle Willie Earl came to see Lula and her new baby.
Aunt Seal said, "oh my!"   "He's such a little thing, but he is so
precious."   Uncle Willie Earl said, "Look at the little fellow."
"I'm going to take him fishing and play ball with him."   Olivia
told Uncle Willie that she would be going back to the house with
them so that she could get cleaned up.   Everyone said their good-
byes to Lula and that they would be back on tomorrow.   Lula got
some rest and Ms. Martha took care of the baby while she slept.
She took a nap from time to time.

The next morning came and Lula had gotten some well-needed
rest.   Ms. Martha started asking her questions and Lula asked
her if her fee was $5.00.   She said yes and asked her where she
lived. Lula started telling her everything that she had been
through.   Ms. Martha told her that she was very fortunate to be
alive and have a man who loved her so much even though he was
not the father of her baby. She also told her that she was sure that
it wouldn't matter to him and all that mattered to him was his love
for her.   Lula said, "Well, I have decided to throw my baby in
the river." "I can't go on like this." "I can't tell Jonathan that
this is his baby. "I can't do it, I can't."   "Look at him. He looks

just like the professor I was telling you about.   Ms. Martha told her, "You know I can't let you throw this baby in the river." "Please don't do it." "PLEASE!"   "I have to talk to my husband," she said. "We don't have any children." "We will take him." "This child is a child of God and we will raise him." "We will keep his name McKinley."   After talking it over with her husband, they both went to Lula and told her that they adopt her son.   Lula said, "That it would make her very happy as school was starting and that she was making plans to get married next month. Lula decided that she would call Jonathan and tell him that she had lost the baby,   but first she would call Aunt Seal and Olivia over to Ms. Martha's. Uncle Willie Earl and Mr. Frank Newton was also there with Aunt Seal, Olivia, and Ms. Martha. Everyone waited to hear what Lula had to say. She sat in a chair ready to leave saying, "I want to finish school and I don't have time for a baby."   "Sooner or later, Jonathan, my fiancé, will find out that this is not his baby, and I just can't take that chance of losing him." "I love Jonathan and I want to make him the happiest man in the world, so I'm letting you all know from heron out, I have lost my baby!"   Olivia gasped for air and Aunt Seal put her head down and said out loud, "are you sure this is what you want?" "You won't be able to change your mind later on."   Ms. Martha said, "Please be sure this is what you want."   Lula said, "Yes. I'm sure."   Aunt Seal had brought over some baby clothes that she had in the house as the baby didn't have anything to wear. Ms.   Martha thanked Aunt Seal.   After she explained her plans, Lula called Jonathan.   He answered the phone saying "hello." "Hi baby" Lula said. Jonathan asked, "Why haven't you called me before now?"   She said, "Say baby. I miscarried."   She then began to cry. Jonathan asked,   "Sweetie, are you alright?" Lula told him that she was a little weak and heartbroken about their baby."   Jonathan asked her when would she be back and told her that he would be waiting at the train station for her. Lula told him that she would be back later on that night. He mentioned that he was so sorry and that he too was also heartbroken about the baby, but that he was more concerned about her and had been worried to death. "I couldn't sleep. Sweetie please give me a number the next time you go somewhere. I was worried sick not knowing."

"You should have had someone call me so that I could have been there for you," Jonathan said. "I'm glad to know that you're alright, I love you, I love and miss you."   Lula told Jonathan that she loved him too and that she would see him later.

Olivia sat there in pure disbelief and said to Lula, "I need to talk to you alone please.   They walked outside and sat on the porch. Olivia said, "you know I feel like we are sisters, I love you too, but I'm going to say this and you may not like me anymore, but what in the hell is wrong with you?" "That is your child, you are his mother, and you can't leave him." "You just can't."   Her eyes were full of tears.   Lula said very quietly, "I know that you may not understand where I'm coming from, but this is my decision and I want you to keep this to yourself". "PLEASE, PLEASE don't tell anyone else, not anyone and especially not Jonathan and please don't tell Oscar."   Olivia agreed to keep her secret saying that "your secret is not mine to tell so I will not say a word." I will be able to see the baby when I come to visit with Aunt Seal.   Olivia helped Lula up off of the stairs. They went back into the house and told Aunt Seal and Uncle Willie Earl that they needed to go.   It was getting late in the day and they needed to leave to get them to the train station.   Lula asked Ms. Martha if she could hold the baby one more time. Ms. Martha handed the baby to her.   She sat down with him and began to cry. She said to the baby, "Now, I could give you anything but life!" "I gave you the name McKinley after my brother."   Most of all, that name came from Vikings." "You are a warrior, a fighter." "You will do well in life! "I pray for you!"   She kissed him and handed him back to his mother, Ms. Martha.   Olivia and Lula walked out the door with Aunt Seal and Uncle Willie Earl and said their good - byes.   They went back into the house and packed their luggage and made it to the train station just in time to get their tickets.   Aunt Seal wanted to talk to Lula before they got on the train.   She took Lula by the hand and sat down next to her looking her in her eyes.   She said to her, "You know there is nothing like a child being raised by its mother." "I also know that God also gives children to the mother that he wants them to be with."

"You were just the transportation for your child to get here."
"The odds were against him as he came early and the fact that you
wanted to throw him away!   "You see our faithful God has to step
in sometimes and make decisions that we have no control over."
Remember that this is God's will."   "This child was meant to
live."   "I have no doubt about it or the mother that God has
chosen for McKinley."   "I have nothing but good things to say
about Ms. Martha and her husband Frank Newton."   "They are
God fearing people."   "So my dear, don't worry because this is
God's will."   "You go on and do great things/"   "I love you and
please don't cry!"   Olivia was sitting close by listening to the
conversation and walked over to Lula and Aunt Seal.   They all
hugged and the train was ready for of the passengers to board..
Lula and Olivia got on and Aunt Seal waited for the train to pull
off.   She waved good - bye to them as the train left.   Lula and
Olivia's ride was very quiet. Lula finally looked over at Olivia
and said, "I just want to thank you for always being here for
me...'   Olivia smiled and they both put their heads together and
gave each other a big hug.   The conductor announced,
"Lorman Mississippi is the next stop."   Lula and Olivia could see
Jonathan and Oscar outside waiting for them.   The conductor
escorted the ladies down as he put out the stepping stool.
Jonathan was right to take Lula's hand. He looked at her from
head to toe saying, "you know you really worried the hell out of
me!" "I have never been so scared." "I didn't know what had
happened."   He also told Lula that he had taken the next few day
off work to take care of her and that he wanted her to come and
stay with him for a few days. She agreed to do so. She really
didn't want to be alone.   She expressed how she felt about the
loss of their baby and how hurt she was.   Olivia was listening
and was frozen in disbelief as she heard what Lula was telling
Jonathan.   Jonathan had called Olivia's name about four times.
Oscar shook her arm very lightly and said, "Olivia baby, what's
wrong?" "Jonathan wanted to say something to you."   Olivia
said, "Oh I'm sorry.   My mind was somewhere else."   "What
was it that you wanted to say?"   Jonathan thanked Olivia for
being there for Lula.   Olivia told him "no problem.   We are like
sisters."   Making it back to drop off Olivia and Oscar,   Jonathan

went to stay with Lula for a few days.   He made it back to his dorm room with Lula, opening up the door to his dorm room with his key.   Lula went inside saying, "Jonathan we have never stayed in your room before... Jonathan said, "Well you know why?"   "It's because of my roommate."   Lula said, "Yes, I know that was the reason."   Jonathan helped Lula put on some pajamas making sure that she was very comfortable.   Both Lula and Jonathan were on the bed and he asked her if she was scared when she lost the baby.   Lula said "yes" and he told her that he was there for her for the rest of their lives.   He held Lula tight for the rest of the night.

Chapter 12

The weekend was approaching and school had already started again. Lula had missed the first week. She vowed that she would be there early the following Monday.   Jonathan was only working part time now.   He also stilled attended morning classes.   He and Lula also had a wedding date to complete. Jonathan asked Lula what she thought about them getting married September 29, as it would be a beautiful Indian summer wedding. Lula told him that that sounded great but that they would just ask family and friends to be there and just keep it small.   Jonathan said, "Well you know my mama." "She will say that she still do things small and the next thing you know there will be thousands of people there."   Lula looked at Jonathan and smiled.   Jonathan told Lula that his mom and dad were really crushed about the loss of their baby and that he thought that it brought his dad to tears. He also mentioned that he had never seen him like that before. Lula put her head down saying, "yes I know."   Lula and Jonathan spent the entire weekend together.   The next week they would be starting back to school.   Monday, the 3rd day of the month was Lula's first day back and her schedule was full this semester as her all of her classes were over two hours each. Lula noticed that her class was very close to Professor Henry Nixon's class.   When her class was over, she walked down the hall passing the door of the professor's classroom.   The professor called out her name asking Lula, Lula is that you?   She turned around and said, "Yes, it's me."   As he walked into his classroom, the professor asked Lula, "Can I please have a word with you in private please?" Lula said, "Okay, sure" as she followed him to his classroom.   The professor looked her up and down and said, "first of all, you look simply amazing!"   "My reason for wanting to talk to you is that you told me that you were pregnant with my child."   "What happened?"   "You don't look like you're having a baby."   As he moved a little closer to her,   Lula said,   "Well for your information, I did have our child."   "You have a son."   "His name is McKinley and I gave him up for adoption."   "I know that you don't give a damn,   I just thought that I would tell you!"

The professor moved a little closer to Lula, rubbed his hand on her face, and kissed her. Lula pulled back, slapped him across the face, and said, "I am engaged to be married!" "You know what marriage is, right?" "Oh I forgot." "You don't have a clue." "Let's get something straight." "This will never happen again." Lula walked away. For the next few weeks, she buried herself into her schoolwork and made plans for her marriage to Jonathan.

September 19th there was breaking news. The weather advisory issued a tropical storm depression warning for the entire southeast part of the United States and for the gulf coast area. Lula and Jonathan paid close attention to the weather especially because of their upcoming plans for the wedding. By the 24th of September, the storm was upgraded to a hurricane. The evening of September 27, everyone had their ears glued to the radio. An announcement came over the radio, "This is the National Broadcasting System." "The hurricane has made its land fall." "Everyone please take shelter!" "Repeat, please take shelter!" "This hurricane had made its land fall in Pascagoula Mississippi, Pensacola Florida, and Mobile Alabama." This was said to be the deadliest and most destructive hurricane in our history. It created nineteen million dollars in damage. The winds were well over 120 miles per hour.

Everyone made it through this horrific ordeal. Jonathan and Lula checked on everyone. Their wedding day was supposed to be today, Saturday, September 29th. Everything was a mess. Jonathan had told his parents that he and Lula would drive to their house to help with the cleanup. They rode out to his parent's house and pulled up in the yard. There were other family members that were also there helping with the cleanup. Trees, branches, and debris were everywhere. Other people roofs had come out of nowhere, animals were lost, and it was very chaotic. Before everyone had gotten started with the cleanup, Jonathan's childhood pastor had come and Pastor Cole was also there. Pastor

Cole gathered everyone together to thank God for sparing them and keeping them covered in the blood of Jesus and gave all praises to God   He ended the prayer by saying "In Jesus's name, Amen!"   The men worked very hard and long.   The women in the house cleaning up the broken windows and putting things back together. Ms.   Jeanette said,   "Lula, I haven't had the time to talk to you, but I am so sorry about the loss of your baby!"   Lula said to Ms.   Jeanette,   "you mean our baby."   Ms.   Jeanette said, "Yeah, y'all baby."   She cleared her throat, changing the subject. Everyone had on their work clothes, not really looking the best. Ms.   Jeanette had made some sandwiches for lunch.   Jonathan went running into the house, grabbed Lula and his mom by the hand, and ran with both of them to the front of the yard where the pastor and his dad were.   Other family members gathered around. Jonathan said,   "Lula, you know that I said that you were going to marry me today."   "The Lord has blessed us to see another day." "The weather was bad,   but it didn't even stop us."   "So this is the day that the Lord has made,   let us rejoice and be glad in it." "Lula Hood,   I don't want to go another day without you becoming my wife."   "Will you give me this today,   to become your husband?   Lula said,   "YES!"   "YES!"   Pastor Cole said, "Well,   let's get started!"   "Dearly beloved.   We are gathered here to join these young people together in holy matrimony." " Jonathan, do you take this woman to be your wife keeping her only for you and forsaking all others from this day forward?" "Until death, do you part?   Jonathan said,   "I do."   Pastor Cole asked Lula,   "Lula Hood,   Do you take this man to be your lawfully wedded husband through sickness and in health,   for better, for richer or poorer,   forsaking all others, till death do you part?"   Lula said,   "I do."   Pastor Cole said,   "Well by the powers invested to me by the state of Mississippi,   I now pronounce you husband and wife."   "You may kiss the bride and jump over the broom!"   The family gathered around them to congratulate the couple.   Ms.   Jeanette walked over to Lula and said,   "Welcome to our family!   Lula hugged her new mother and father - in - law very tight.   Lula and Jonathan continued to help putting things back together.   They made sure that everything went smooth.   It was getting late in the day.   Joseph Brooks had called everyone over to the front of the yard.   He wanted to make an announcement to make a toast of good health,   good wealth, and many grandchildren.   He said,   "most of all,   I want to give you and my new daughter - in - law some land - so that you can build your family a home.   He showed the couple where the land was.   It was about 50 yards away from Jonathan's parent's home. Lula and Jonathan were so very appreciative of Joseph's good gesture.   They gave him a big.   Jonathan said to his dad with tears in his eyes,   "thank you dad!"   "We will get started building very very soon,   but tonight,   I'm going to carry my wife home." "I know that we don't live together yet,   but I know that God will make a way for us.   "So,   Mr. & Mrs. Jonathan Brooks will be back soon to start building.   They told everyone good night, got into the truck, and went back to Lula's dorm room.   The dorms and the school had not been damaged in the hurricane.   Jonathan carried Lula up the stairs,   opened up the door,   walked across the doorway, and said, "Jump over the threshold."   "You are my wife and I truly love you."   "I'm so glad that you gave me the honor of being your husband."   "When I wake up every morning,   I will be graced with your beauty and I feel our heart beat on one accord...   'You are so sweet, kind, loyal,   honest, and faithful." " You are my everything."   Lula said,   "Yes sweetie."   "Our marriage will be built on trust and honesty from this day forth. "Our marriage means the world to me."   Lula started to think about the baby in her mind and thought if she was being honest, thinking what Jonathan didn't know wouldn't hurt him.   She thought in her mind,   "Besides,   we didn't get serious until after I was pregnant."   She also thought about the first time she and Jonathan had gone out on a date and all that mattered was her love for him now.   Lula and Jonathan spent the next few days consummating their marriage.   They also concentrated on school making sure that they were passing classes this semester.

Chapter 13

For the next three months, every Saturday Jonathan and Lula were breaking ground building their new house with the help of family and friends.   The very first week was spent laying the foundation. All of the men were outside taking part in all of the labor.   All of the women who came to help were inside to help with the cooking, making curtains, and crocheting comforters for Jonathan and Lula.   The ladies had good conversations.   Some young lady had asked Lula if she wasn't pregnant and wanted to know what had happened.   Lula told her that it was very painful but that she had a miscarriage and that she and Jonathan were healing and that God would heal everything and would bless them with another child. The young lady said,   "Yes God will work it out."

Chapter 14

After the end of the three months, their beautiful home was all done.   Everyone came together on the last Saturday to put the final touches on everything making sure the windows were all in place and the doors were on right.   It was a nice one-story house with a fireplace and 3 bedrooms.   All of Jonathan and Lula's family and friends were on the porch and in the yard.   Jonathan opened up the door, turned to his wife, and said to her, "wait a minute."   He picked her up in his arms, said, "This is our home" and carried her across the threshold.   Lula turned to Jonathan and said, "I have some news"   "We are having a baby!" Jonathan asked, "Really?"   Lula said,   "YES!'   "YES!" Jonathan was so happy.   He did a dance and turned to Lula and hugged her very tight.   The family and friends went into the house and took a tour of their new home.   Everyone was so very happy.   The year 1906 was coming to an end and Lula and Jonathan had gone through so much.   They had been married for only three months and were concerned as they were both big on education.   Lula wanted her husband to speak with their family and friends about their education and how Jonathan planned on going into law and Lula being a teacher.   Their open house would be Saturday January 5, 1907.

Chapter 15

The time had come for the open house.   All of their family and
friends had gathered to share in the celebration.   There was so
much food, singing, laughter, and enjoying one another.   Jonathan
started to speak and express their gratitude thanking everyone for
their help in building their home. He said, "I just want everyone
to know that I'm willing to help in building for anyone who needs
me."   He also let everyone know how far they had come as black
people. He said,   "You know that it was Frederick Douglass who
paved the way for our freedom and civil rights."   "He gave me
inspiration through his work."   "He was born a slave in the year
of 1818 in the county of Talbot Maryland."   'You know
Frederick Douglass was most famous for his intellectuals, lecturing
to thousands on so many different causes, and standing up for
women's rights. He had become a free man in the year of 1838,
kept black families aware of both their past and present,   was an
abolitionist, journalist, and author. "   "So, my wife and I want
you all to know that we are going to build a school house in this
community.   "My wife, Mrs. Lula Brooks, formerly known as
Ms. Lula Hood, will be one of the founding teachers..."   "If
anyone want to be a part of the school, please let me know.   "We
also would need any input regarding this situation."   Everyone
began to clap.   Ms. Jeanette and Joseph were so proud of both of
them.   They also let the family know with excitement how they
would need all of their help in making this work.   The day was
getting late and Lula and Jonathan walked their friends and family
to their vehicles and saw them off as they listened to their idea
about the new school that was going to be built in the
neighborhood.

Chapter 16

The next six months Lula had gotten so big with her pregnancy. It was almost exactly a year later from giving birth to McKinley. It was Monday, June 24, 1907 when Lula went into labor.   She was up making her husband some breakfast.   They both would always sit and eat breakfast together.   Jonathan was done eating and turned around to give Lula a goodbye kiss.   He would always hug his wife before leaving for the day.   Looking down at the floor, he could see Lula standing in a puddle of water.   Jonathan said, "Baby are you alright?"   "Is it time for our baby?"   Lula said, "Yes sweetie, I believe so."   "I've been in labor and have been having cramps all night."   Jonathan asked his wife why she didn't say something.   He said, "I don't want to lose our baby and most of all, I don't want to lose you."   "I need to be with you." Lula started to say something but she was distracted by the pain. Her contractions were getting worse and the pain was more frequent.   At this point, Jonathan was getting more frantic.   Lula had to calm him down.   She said very slowly, "sweetie go over to your parents' house and tell them we need their help.   Jonathan said "okay."   He was gone only a few minutes and came rushing back to the door with his parents.   Ms. Jeanette said to her son, "baby go get the truck."   Jonathan's parents helped Lula walk to the truck and assisted her in getting inside.   They drove to the hospital, South Central Hospital on Jefferson Street.   Jonathan's parents followed close behind them.   Once there, Jonathan got out of the truck to help his wife inside.   He was holding his wife as they walked to the counter in the waiting room.   Jonathan said to the receptionist, "my wife is having our baby."   The receptionist said, "Let me get the nurse."   "I will get all of the information from your husband and the nurse will be out here soon to take you back to your room."   The nurse took Lula back to one of the labor rooms.   Jonathan's parents walked in the door right after Lula had left the waiting room.   Ms. Jeanette asked, "Where is she?" Jonathan told her that they had taken her back already and his mom and dad said, "okay we will just wait out here with you son." Jonathan paced the floor waiting for news on the condition of his wife and their baby. Lula was now in some very hard labor. The nurse returned to the waiting room to give an update on Lula's contractions. 'Her labor continued for thirty plus hours. Jonathan had fallen asleep, as he was exhausted. After he had been asleep for a few hours, it was time. The nurse came out and said to Jonathan, "Mr. Brooks your wife and new baby are resting." "Your wife is in her room and your baby is in the nursery." "Okay!" "Is my baby a girl or a boy?" "I will let your wife tell you," the nurse said. Jonathan walked in the room to see Lula. He leaned over and kissed his wife saying you look so beautiful. Lula smiled, still tired from giving birth to their new baby. Jonathan asked her, well do we have a baby girl or is it a boy? Lula said, "We have a baby boy." Jonathan jumped for joy. "Yes I'm a daddy" he said, and asked, "When can I see my son?" Lula told Jonathan, "He's in the nursery. Jonathan went to the waiting room to get is parents. He said to both of them, "Mama, daddy, it's a boy." "Come on so we can go to see him." They stood outside the nursery and saw the name "Brooks Baby" on the nametag. Jonathan saw his son for the first time and tears started running down his face. His parents gave Jonathan a big hug. Jonathan said, "He is so beautiful..." "Look they say that he weighed eight pounds." His father said, "now that is a really big baby!' All three of them stood at the window of the nursery smiling and blowing kisses to the new baby. Jonathan tapped on the window to talk to the nurse. He wanted to hold his son. The nurse told him that he would have to put on a gown and a mask so that the baby wouldn't get sick. The nurse opened up the door to let him in. She held the baby in her hands and told Jonathan, here is your son. She also asked him if he and his wife had thought of a name for their son. Jonathan said, "Not yet." "I haven't had the chance to talk it over with my wife." He held his son for the first time. His parents were still on the other side of the nursery looking at their grandson. Jonathan smiled from ear to ear and his mom and dad smiled too.

Later on, Jonathan returned to Lula's hospital room. He leaned over and kissed Lula again. He asked her, what name do we have in mind for our son?   Lula said, "what about naming him Jonathan Joseph Brooks or Jonathan SR?"   Jonathan tried to hold back his tears of joy.   He said, "I think that you forgot something.   Lula asked, "What?"   "There is only one Jonathan SR, so he will be Jonathan Joseph the second.   She agreed saying "yes the second."   "You are one sweetie."   Jonathan told everyone, we have that all taken care of now.   Ms. Jeanette asked Lula how she was feeling.   Lula said that she was a little tired but very happy.   Ms. Jeanette said, "Well you need your rest."   "Your father - in - law have been here from the time you first came."   We're tired too."   We're so happy with our new grandson."   "So give me a big kiss and hug."   " I will be back to see you real soon.   Ms. Jeanette and Mr.   Joseph said their good byes and went home.   Jonathan and Lula spent the rest of the night sleeping.   Lula rested in the hospital bed.   Jonathan just couldn't leave her and the baby.   He slept in the waiting room.

For the next three days, Lula, Jonathan, and the new baby all rested as a family at the hospital.   Now it was time to go home as Lula and the baby had been discharged.   It was a very hot day. Jonathan had gone to get the truck and the nurse was escorting Lula and baby Jonathan to the door.   The new daddy got out of the truck to help his wife and son get in.   The nurse held the baby while Jonathan helped his wife Lula up in the truck.   The nurse handed the baby to the new mother and wished the family a good life.   They arrived back home and family and friends made them feel so welcome.   Ms. Jeanette had gotten together with everyone to make sure that the new parents didn't need anything as far as baby clothes or a baby bassinet.   Lula wanted to breast feed her son to make sure that he was getting his nourishment.   With all of the excitement of the new baby, Ms. Jeanette had to put an end to the visitors at her son and daughter - in - law's home.   She said to all of the visitors, "I'm so happy that everyone is enjoying the new baby!"   "I know that my son won't say anything, so I will." "We must let them get their rest."   "We all have this weekend for the big announcement."   Ms. Jeanette made sure that Lula and Jonathan were all settled in and left going home for the night.

The weekend had finally arrived.   Jonathan had gotten up bright and early on Saturday morning.   He was telling his wife that he had a very big surprise.   He explained to Lula that his mom and dad would come over to watch the baby.   He wanted to take her somewhere special and asked her to put something on real nice. Jonathan had gotten Lula up in the truck and they were on their way to this big event.   Lula had been so busy with the birth of their child and hadn't been concentrating on the effort of the schoolhouse that was being built.   They arrived at the new school.   The school was small, but it was built all in honor of his lovely wife.   Jonathan said to Lula, "baby are you excited?" Lula said "yes!" There were many other people there to celebrate. It was only a two-room schoolhouse.   The weather was very warm as it was well into 90 degrees.   There was an announcer who made a little speech.   The gentleman said, "We are opening up this new school in this area in honor of Mrs.   Lula Hood Brooks."   Next, the sign was unveiled with Lula's name on it. Lula was speechless and was brought to tears.   The announcer introduced her to speak.   She made her way to the front of the crowd and said to everyone, "I just want to thank everyone for making me the very first teacher of our new school."   "I know that it is named after me and I take this honor with so much pride." "I want you to know that my educational background is very important to me and that I also believe in the students of Brook Side community."   "The state of Mississippi's corporal punishment law is very common for students enrolled in K- 12th grades."   "The children of Mississippi are disciplined at a higher percentage than any other state and racial segregation is very prevalent in our state."   "We have been ranked last on the list year after year and with that being said, Mississippi's poorest residents are children of color."   "Twenty four percent of the families who live in our state live in poverty."   "So, I am very proud to say that it really takes a village to raise a child and that I really hope to make a difference in the education of the children in our community."   "I'm looking forward to the children of this community attending this wonderful school in the fall of this year. There was a nice lunch and open house so that everyone could enjoy the celebration.

Chapter 17

The fall of 1907 marked the beginning of the new school year. The parents of the children in the surrounding area came to make sure there was room for them in the new school.   This wasn't an easy job for Lula, as she would be teaching about 20 students from kindergarten through 12th graders.   She loved the fact that she would be close to her own home, which was about four blocks away.   She wanted to be close to her son.   Ms. Jeanette would watch her grandson.   Women working outside of the home was really unheard of.   Some women didn't have a husband in the home and men were never seen around their houses.   Yet somehow, year after year, children kept being born.   So mothers had to be both parents in a child's life.   A lot of children would help out working in the fields. On Lula's first day of school,   she stood before the children and said, "good morning class." "My name is Mrs. Brooks and I will be teaching all of you."   "I see that I will need an assistant and will decide who that person will be."   "We have two classrooms and I will be separating you all by how far you are in your education."   "Don't be ashamed or discouraged as you can move up to a higher level."   "I will pass out a small test to determine the grade level each of you are on." "She also explained that the classroom might also be broken up into four sections and before they could go any further, she wanted to make sure that they all were familiar with The Pledge of Allegiance.   One of the students raised her hand.   Lula said, "Yes Susan."   Susan stood up and said, "The Pledge of Allegiance was written by Francis Bellamy in the year of 1892."   Lula said, "Well Susan, could you lead the class in reciting the pledge?" Susan agree to do so and the class started saying the pledge too. Lula told the class that they would recite the pledge each morning. She also asked Susan if she would pass the test papers to each student in order to know which grade level to place each student in.   She could see immediately that Susan stood out as a highly advanced student and that she would be her assistant.   She would also make sure that Susan would be challenged also further her own education.   For the next few months, Lula was very busy as a teacher, wife, and mother.   The semester had come and gone. The New Year was fast approaching.

Chapter 18

The new year of 1908 had come and Jonathan and Lula had a nice quiet night together. They spent quality time listening to the radio about big city life. The announcer was giving a clear description of the entertainment that was going on in New York City. When people talked about the north and the city of New York, you didn't hear about the wide spread of racism. This was the first time for the Big Ball of light to be dropped down from a flagpole into the crowd in New York City in Time Square in 1908. It seemed like everyone loved each other and that there weren't any walls of discrimination. Lula and Jonathan played music and listened to the Soul Jazz as they were in love, loving life, and enjoying their son. 1908 was a leap year. There were a number of lynching's in the state of Mississippi for no apparent reason. It really triggered something deep in Lula's soul knowing that was how her father was killed. This made Lula afraid for her husband and both of her sons. However, many people didn't know about her oldest son as she had given him up for adoption. She always had McKinley on her mind and wondered how he was doing. Lula talked to herself and said, "I could call Aunt Seal to find out how he's doing." "I'm going to call tomorrow and wish them a blessed new year and many many more to come." In the meantime, both Lula and Jonathan thanked God for all that he had done for them. After thanking him for blessing them with a new son, they went to bed for the night and held each other.

They both concentrated on furthering their education as the New Year had arrived. They both attended college. Lula attended one day out of the week. She was able to start teaching as she already had both associates and bachelor degrees, and was now working on her master's degree. Her classroom assistant, Susan, held things down while she attended her class. She still attended Alcorn University and had one class every Wednesday from one o'clock pm until three o'clock pm. Jonathan attended there also and Lula would wait on him to ride home with her husband. She waited for him in the cafeteria most of the time.   She caught up on her assignments and thought on and developed creative ideas for her young students while she waited for him.   She noticed Mr. Henry Nixon sitting across the room one Wednesday while she waited on Jonathan.   She ignored his presence. Professor Nixon walked over to the table where she was sitting and said, "Hello beautiful." Lula looked up and said, "good afternoon." He asked if he could have a seat and Lula said, "Yes you may." The professor said that he wanted to talk to her for a moment because she told him that he had a son out in the world and he wanted to know about him.   He told her that he knew that she was very busy but needed to know if she could meet him next week in his classroom.   He also asked her which day would be good for her. Lula said that she didn't know and asked why he wanted to know about him now. She explained that the child was over 18 months old.   The professor said that he wasn't sure why but that the child had been on his mind. Lula stood up and told the professor that she would be at his classroom the next week on Wednesday at three thirty pm.   The professor said that he was looking forward to seeing her. Lula refused to say anything and walked away.   Lula was thinking what could he want to do with this information? Knowing that she didn't lose her baby, she couldn't let Jonathan find out about this.   She remembered that she had thought about calling Aunt Seal to check on her son. Jonathan picked his wife up and they drove home.   Lula asked her husband to please pick up their son from his parents' house He said that he would. She needed to make a phone call and knew that her in laws were long winded and that Jonathan would be tied up in a conversation with them for a while. Lula placed the call to Aunt Seal.   The phone rang about four times and Aunt Seal answered. Lula said, "Hello, this is Lula." Lula asked how are you and Uncle Willie Earl? She also said that she was curious and wanted to know how baby McKinley was doing.   "Oh hi sweetie" Aunt Seal said. "The baby is doing fine, he's getting so big and child, he is so handsome." "I tell you he is so smart and I see him every Sunday at church."   Lula said, "Well I hope to come and visit soon!   Aunt Seal said, "Well make sure that you do that!" "I'm not getting any younger," Aunt Seal said. "Okay, I have to go now, but I want to wish you a happy new year." "I know that I'm a few weeks late telling you, but you are always on my mind and in my heart." "I will talk to you soon." Aunt Seal said, "Okay, I'll talk to you soon." As Lula hung up the phone, Jonathan and Jr. were coming through the door. Jonathan was being playful with and talking baby talk to his son. Lula was so happy to see her son. She gave him big hugs and kisses. Jonathan & Lula made preparations for the next day and to make it through the next week.

The following Wednesday had finally come. Lula had told Professor Nixon that she would come to see him to discuss their son. It was 3:25 pm and she walked to the professor's classroom and knocked on the door. The professor said, "Come in." Lula went in the room. Professor Nixon said, "Please, please close the door." "I don't want anyone to disturb us and I want and need your undivided attention." The professor walked over to the light switch. Lula asked what are you doing? The professor said to Lula, "I miss you!" Lula stood there and her feet couldn't move. The professor locked the door taking Lula by the hand. He pulled her closer to him. They both looked each other in their eyes. Neither one pulled away from each other. The professor took his hand and slid it down her face. He said to Lula, "you are stunning. I have never met a woman of your style and beauty." Lula said, "thank you. " "I thought that you wanted to know about your son." The professor said, "Yes I want to know." "You know that you miss me." "Tell me that you don't want me!" Lula said, "I'm happily married!" Professor Nixon said, "Okay, you are free to walk out the door anytime." Lula said, "Okay let's cut to the chase!" "I wanted you to know that your son live in Vicksburg Mississippi, he was adopted as I couldn't take care of him, and you knew that." The professor stood in his classroom with this big smile on his face. Lula came in and had a seat. He walked over and grabbed Lula by the hand. He placed his hand on her heart. She closed her eyes and laid her head on his shoulder. The two of them started to kiss and one thing led to another. Before they knew it, they were undressed. The professor looked admiring Lula's body. Lula did the unthinkable, making love to the professor once again. Lula had forgotten the fact that she was married during her moment of passion. They both got dressed. Lula knew that Jonathan would be here to pick her up soon. She hurried leaving out of the professor's classroom, not even saying good-bye to him. She saw Jonathan waiting for her in the cafeteria. She asked him if he had been waiting on her for a long time. Jonathan asked her, "Sweetie, are you okay?" Lula said, "Yes." Jonathan told her that she looked a bit disheveled. She said that she had been outside and that some kind of bird must have thought that her hair looked like a nest and got in her hair. She also told him that she was trying to fight the bird off. Jonathan took his wife by the hand, walked her to the truck, and they drove home. Arriving home, they settled down for the evening, and sat at the dinner table. Jonathan asked her again if she was okay. Lula said, "Yes, of course I'm fine." "I just have a lot of things on my mind as I'm teaching, going to school, am concerned about our baby." "I don't want to neglect our child." Jonathan asked her, what do you want to do?" Lula said that she had made up her mind to strop going to class for a while and would go back later on in life. She explained that he and the baby were her life and that she needed to give them her undivided attention. Jonathan said, "WOW!" "What brought this on?" "Whatever you want, I want. Too." "I just want to make sure that you are truly happy sweetheart." "I love you and our son." Lula said, "I'm just tired." "That's all. They finished their dinner and Lula cleaned the kitchen and put the food away. Jonathan played with the baby and got him ready for bed. By that time, Lula was finished with everything. She made herself some bath water, got inside of the bathtub, and couldn't think of anything else except relaxing. As she was soaking in the water, she started thinking in her mind about what had happened with the professor. She couldn't believe that she had broken her vows! She asked herself, "Why did I do it?" Jonathan called out to Lula, "baby you've been in the tub for a long time." "Are you coming to bed?" "Yes, I'll be there shortly" Lula said. She got out of the tub, dried herself off, and put her gown on. Jonathan was already in bed waiting for her. She got in bed with her husband and he got behind her holding, hugging, and kissing her on her neck. Lula just laid there kind of motionless. Jonathan tried to caress her breasts, but she pulled away slightly. She showed her husband clearly that she wasn't interested at all in making love to him. Jonathan asked her, what's going on? Why are you being so distant from me? You need to tell me something because I'm not understanding. Lula said, "Baby I'm just exhausted." "I get up at the crack of dawn and I need some rest." "That's why I'm going to finish up with my class this semester." "I will have more time for us. Baby, I hope that you understand." "Okay, I understand," said Jonathan. He held Lula in his arms for the rest of the night and they both fell fast asleep

Chapter 19

For the next three months, Jonathan and Lula had gotten closer, making love to one another.   Lula had dropped her class at the college for now.   But she still had Professor Nixon on her mind. She knew that she had made a mistake with her indiscretions. Lula loved her husband.   She had some news to tell Jonathan this particular morning.   The both of them would always start their day together with breakfast and would always end their day with dinner.   Lula was sitting at the table drinking some coffee.   She said to her husband, "I'm pregnant again!"   Jonathan said, "Really?" "How long have you known this information?"   Lula said, "oh, maybe about a week." "I just really wanted to make sure that I was pregnant."   Jonathan said, "Well, Jr. Is not even one year old." "Baby I'm just concerned about your happiness and your wellbeing.   Lula looked at Jonathan and began to cry. Jonathan walked over to her and started kissing and hugging her. He also told her how much he loved her. He said, "I know that you have only known for a week that you are pregnant, so how many months do you think that you are?"   Lula said, "I believe that I am approximately four months.   Jonathan said, "Well, we will get through this just like we have done everything else." "Oh sweetie, stop crying."   The next four and a half months were very intimate for Jonathan and Lula.   She kept the facts of her infidelity to herself and never told a soul.   The only two people who knew were she and Professor Henry Nixon.   She wasn't sure who could be the father of her unborn baby!   She said, "that when she did go into labor, she wanted go back to Vicksburg Mississippi to Ms. Newton, the midwife.   Jonathan said that he had no problem with the midwife as long as he would be there.   Lula had called Mrs. Martha Newton to ask her permission to come.   Ms. Martha said, "Yes, don't forget the cost which is $5.00 to deliver a baby." Lula said, "Yes Ma'am.   I will come that way when I go into labor." Ms. Martha said, "That's great. We look forward to seeing you soon."   She told Ms. Martha, "I'm bringing my husband, so please make sure that he knows nothing about my son McKinley." "I told my husband that my first born had died in childbirth."   Ms.

Martha said that she remembered and besides that, the child was now hers. Lula said, "Yes, he is." She was also asking Ms. Martha a favor and said, " I know I have no right in asking you this and I know that it was me who had no regards for life because I wanted to throw my child in the river." "I just can ask God to forgive me for my action and I know that it was only God who put you in McKinley's life." "It was God's master plan Ms. Martha that he put you in his life." " I know that we may never really look back and truly understand the power of God's plan, but I can only ask that because of my past. Please instill in McKinley three things." "First, to always put God first, second, to put family next, and third, to make sure to get an education."   "Please make sure that you help him to get his education." Ms. Martha said, "Yes those are my same values and I will do that..." They both hung up the phone. Lula knew that the time was near to give birth to her third child. She started cleaning and putting things in order so that when the time came, she would be ready. She had a suitcase all packed and also had things ready for her son Junior as she knew that he would be cared for by her mother-in-law, Mrs. Jeanette. Night had finally come and Lula was resting in her husband's arms all night. The next morning was such a bright and beautiful day! You could hear the sound of the birds singing, smell the smell of the mountain dew, feel the cool breeze of fresh air, and see the flowers blooming. There was also the quietness of peace and it felt as though there was nothing but you and God. Lula was thanking God for this wonderful life. She was just sitting there on her porch at home. Jonathan and the baby were sleeping. Jonathan came out, put his head over Lula's shoulder, kissing his wife, saying "good morning my love! Lula said, "good morning: and she kissed him back sharing in the beautiful morning. Jonathan said to Lula, "From the very first day that I laid my eyes on you, I was smitten by your beauty, your style, and your grace." "I knew that you were sent to me by God!" "I just want to thank him for each and every day of our lives."   Lula looked at Jonathan and told him, "You were also sent to me from God. You are my best friend, my strength mentally, physically, and spiritually, always putting God first." 'You know we all fall short of the glory of God."   "Yes we do, we have all done something that we are not proud of" Jonathan said.   Lula said, "Yes, so very true."   It was now time for breakfast.   Lula gave Jonathan a kiss and walked back into the kitchen to prepare her family a wonderful breakfast of thick bacon, homemade biscuits, and fresh sunny side up eggs.   When she was done cooking, she went into the bedroom to get her son Junior.   They all sat down to breakfast as a family.   Junior was at the age of getting into a little bit of everything. Lula looked across the table at her husband and said, "If anything happens to me, I need you to promise me that you will make sure that Junior gets his education. "   "I don't know what sex the child will be, but please take care of it." Jonathan told Lula that she knew that he was almost done with his schooling and he vowed to make their lives a better one; one better than his parents, his grandparents, and the things that they went through.   He said, "Let me talk about how far we have come as people (Black people)." "You know that the state of Mississippi is known for having the largest amount of slaves in the country." "Mississippi is also known as being the number one place to grow cotton. So you know what happened to all of the slaves when they were set free."   They still found themselves bound to the same land in which they were enslaved.   This went on for generation-to-generation only keep black families poor and in poverty.   These families would work the fields doing the hard work for the landowner.   When they tried to make a profit for their family, the owner would tell them that they had to stay on their land for free. So, the sharecropper would have to also feed his family, which resulted in him doing the work without any kind of profit.   He said, "So sweetheart, I know how important it is for our future generations to better themselves"   Lula said to her husband, "I can now relax after just hearing you say this to me." "All of our hard work will pay off in the future of our children.   When we are no longer here on this earth knowing that what we instilled in our children would help them benefit from generation to generation. They will have a bright future it would be like looking out to the sea and not being able to see where it will take you or what truly there until you get to the other side."   Lula said to Jonathan, "I don't know what has gotten into me this morning. I just know that it is a very beautiful day and I'm going to go and take a nice nap."

Jonathan told her that sounded like a good idea as she had been up
early that day and that he would take Junior with him while she
rested.   Lula said, "Okay."   Later on that evening, Lula started
having cramps and told Jonathan that she thought that it was time
for them to make their way to Vicksburg Mississippi to Ms.
Martha's, the midwife's house.   Jonathan was all-nervous asking
her questions. He asked,   "Do you have your suitcase ready,
and what about the baby's things to take to our parents' house?
She said "yes" and Jonathan said, "Okay, I will take the baby over
to mom and dads now."   Lula said, "Okay, but wait a moment.
I need to kiss my baby and tell him that I love him before we go."
Jonathan agreed and told her that she was acting as though she
wasn't coming back.   Lula looked at him and told him, "you
know its God's will and we never know what may happen"
Jonathan agreed saying, "You're right."   Put his arms around her
and the baby, and said,   "I love you so much!"   She sat there in
a chair waiting for him to take the baby over to his parents.
Making his way back, he asked if she was ready.   She said "not
yet. I need to call Ms. Martha and let her know that we are on
our way." Jonathan agreed saying, "Okay." After making the
call, she told her husband that she was ready.   Jonathan helped
her into the truck and they were ready to leave.   It wasn't dark yet
and they were approximately an hour away from Vicksburg.
Jonathan looked over to Lula and asked her if she was alright.
She looked at him holding his hand and said, "I'm doing fine."
Jonathan started praying and singing to try to make things better.
Lula was very quiet and Jonathan told her that they were almost
there.   She looked at him and started to cry.   Jonathan told her,
"baby it's going to be okay" and Lula said,   "I hope so." "I know
that I have been very emotional this week."   She tried to show
Jonathan the way to Martha and Frank Newton's house.   They
finally made it there and it was dark outside. Jonathan got out
first and knocked on the door. Ms. Martha said,   "Hi, I'm
ready for you."   "Her bed is made up."   Jonathan went to the
truck to get his wife.   He walked her up the three stairs to the door
into the room where she would give birth to their baby.   Ms.
Martha said to Lula,   "let me help you get a bath and into a nice
gown so that you can get comfortable."   Jonathan sat on the sofa

while Ms. Martha helped his wife.   Ms.   Martha's husband came out of the bedroom as he heard the commotion going on in his house.   Frank Newton reached out his hand to shake Jonathan's hand. Jonathan said,   "My name is Jonathan and Lula is my wife..."   Mr. Newton said, "I'm very pleased to meet you. He asked Jonathan if he could offer him a drink of cold ice tea. Jonathan told him yes that he would love to have a drink.   Both of the men were sitting on the porch talking about life in general. Jonathan turned and saw a little boy standing in the doorway.   He was awakened by the activities going on in the house.   Jonathan said, "hi little man" and asked Mr.   Frank Newton,   "is this your son?"   Frank said "yes" and Jonathan asked, "How old is he?"   Frank told him that the child was almost two years old. Frank told Jonathan that he would have to excuse him for the moment while he put McKinley back to bed.   Jonathan was thinking, WOW!   That's Lula's brother's name.   What are the chances of that also, Jonathan's mind started to wonder. He thought about two years ago when Lula said that she lost their child in childbirth as he was still born.   He said to himself, "Okay, let me get my mind straight and concentrate on the reason we are here." "I will ask that question later on.   Ms. Martha came out to the porch to let Jonathan know that his wife was ready to see him and said,   "I have her comfortable for now, you can go back and keep her company, and also the bed is big enough if you want to sleep with your wife. She also told him that for right then, she was going to catch a nap as it was going to be a long night and maybe also the next day."   Jonathan thanked her and Ms. Martha told him that he was welcome and told him good night and not to hesitate to come and get her if he needed her.   Jonathan said that he would and went back to where Lula was resting.   He saw Lula trying to stay asleep but her contractions just kept waking her up. He laid by her holding on to her with every pain that she had. These contractions were about ten minutes apart and continued throughout the night.

It was finally morning and Lula was still in so much pain.   Ms. Martha came to the door, knocked on it, and asked how Lula was doing.   She let her know that it was time for her to check her internally to see if the baby was close to being born.   Jonathan said that he would step outside for a minute. Ms. Martha checked on Lula and said that her water had not broken and that the labor could continue for another day.   She also told Lula that she hadn't had any rest, things didn't look good, and that she thought that she should go to the local hospital.   Lula said, "Not yet."   "I'm really too tired to go anywhere." Ms. Martha told her that if she waited too late, she and her baby could die!   Lula didn't say a word and fell back to sleep briefly only to be awakened by the pain of her contractions.   It was getting worst. Finally, her water had broken as she was going to the bathroom. She was not strong enough to go to the outhouse, which was the only bathroom there.   Lula used a slop jar.   As she went to use the bathroom, a gush of water came down, and she could hear a popping sound. Ms. Martha said, "That was a great sign" and Lula had to be cleaned up again.   Ms. Martha helped her get comfortable again.   Lula tried to rest, but wasn't able to do so. Ms.   Martha continued checking her vagina to see if she had made any changes.   The contractions were unbearable and Lula laid in all of this pain.   She turned to look at the door for a moment.   There stood McKinley, just a little fellow.   They both made eye contact.   Lula cried out in pain and McKinley walked over to her holding on to her finger.   Lula stopped moving. There was no movement. The crying out had stopped.   Both Jonathan and Ms.   Martha walked back into the room and saw McKinley holding Lula's hand and that it was not moving. Jonathan called out her name and there was no response. He called out her name, "Lula!" "Lula!"   He put his head to her chest and didn't hear her heart beating anymore! He also cried and held her so close to him.   Ms.   Martha asked if she could help her. Jonathan wouldn't let go of her and held her for about three to four hours before taking his arms from around his wife. Ms. Martha felt so devastated about the situation and told Jonathan how sorry she was and that she did check Lula to find out the reason for her losing her life.   She said that the baby was breached.   Jonathan asked her to explain what she meant by the word breached.   Ms. Martha explained that sometimes the baby was in a bottom first position meaning that the baby was trying to come out feet or bottom first which makes it very difficult for the child to be born. She continued to say, "I am so very sorry!" "I know that it is very hard." "If you would like, my husband and I can help you transport your wife's body to the funeral home of your choice." Jonathan told her that he would appreciate their help and that he guessed that he needed to make a few phone calls as he wanted to first call his mom and dad and that they or he would call the funeral home in his city. Ms. Martha asked for the name of the funeral home and Jonathan said The Chapel of Angels Funeral Home would be used. He asked Ms. Martha to allow him to get himself together while he made the phone call. The phone rang. Jonathan's mama picked up the phone and said, "Hello." He said, "Mama" and began to cry. Mrs. Jeanette asked, "Baby 'what is wrong?' "Mama, Lula didn't make it." "She just died" Jonathan said. Ms. Jeanette let out a big scream and a loud cry! By that time, Jonathan's dad was on the phone saying, "son what's wrong with your mother?" "She is so full of tears right now and I can't make any sense of her conversation." Jonathan told his dad, "daddy Lula died in giving birth to our child. "They say the baby was breached." "I will explain to you later on and I need you like never before.' "I will transport her body back to The Chapel of Angels Funeral Home. Jonathan's dad said, "Okay son. I'm here for you, I love you, and it's going to be alright." Jonathan told his dad "okay" as he hung up the phone. Ms. Martha told Jonathan that she would call Aunt Seal to let her know what happened and to see if Frank and Uncle Willie Earl could help with the transportation. She also told him that someone could drive his truck while he made sure that his wife's remains were being transported respectfully. Jonathan agreed. The ride was very emotional for Jonathan. Lula's body was in the truck with Frank and Jonathan. They sat her body right next to Jonathan as they made that long and sad hour drive to the funeral home. As they made it to The Chapel of Angels Funeral Home, it was very hard for Jonathan to say good-bye. The funeral director met them at the door to receive Lula's body. He told Jonathan that he could go home and get himself together if he would like to and come back later to make final arrangements for his wife. He realized that this would be a very hard thing for Jonathan to go through. He also said, "but we here at The Chapel of Angels are here to make this unexpected situation a respectful and caring one for your loved one. Jonathan thanked him and said that he would be back soon to make final arrangements. The funeral director told him that he would see him when he returned.

Jonathan went back to his mom and dad's house. Arriving there, his mom and dad went out to greet their son. They tied to hold everything together, but everyone had broken down crying. Jonathan asked his parents, as he really needed to see him. His mom told him that his son was in the house with his auntie. Jonathan entered the house and took his son in his arms and held him like there was no tomorrow. Jonathan's auntie told him, "baby I am so sorry." He looked at her and said "thank you." He took his son and left to go to their home. He stood on the porch with his son. His feet wouldn't let him move to open the door. He held back the tears as he walked inside the house. Jonathan knew that he needed to get himself cleaned up and to try and stay focused. But he couldn't help but reminisce about the last time that they were in the house together. He told himself to stay focused as he looked around the house to find their insurance policy. Jonathan found a metal box under the bed containing the insurance policy for five thousand dollars. It also contained a letter to Jonathan. His name was on the front of the envelope written in Lula's handwriting. Jonathan took the letter to the kitchen, sat down, and opened it. The letter read "my dearest Jonathan. If you're reading this letter, it could only mean one or two things." "Either I'm very ill or I am no longer here on this earth." "Sweetheart please don't grieve for me too long." "I know how much you have loved me and I LOVED YOU TOO." "Please remarry when you can." "You are the best husband God could have ever given me." "I need to tell you something that you may not understand." "You know before I met you, I had been having a sexual relationship with one of the professors at our college at Alcorn University." "When I first met you that was one of the last times that the professor and I had been intimate. " "I had no idea that I was pregnant by the professor." "Then God sent me you and baby I didn't know what to do." "Yes, the child is alive and he lives with Ms. Martha and her husband Frank Newton." "I'm so sorry for you to find out this way, but I just didn't know how to tell you." "Please know that I will love you for all eternity!" "Until I see you again, my love, Lula Hood Brooks."

Jonathan sat there in disbelief and said to himself, "WOW!" About an hour later, he went back to the funeral home to make all of the arrangements. He met with the funeral director and went over everything. The arrangements were all taken care of. The funeral was scheduled for a week from that day. Jonathan's family came to give him so much love and comfort. They came from near and far.

One week later, they all met to say good-bye to his beloved wife. The funeral was held in The Jonathan Family Church and everyone met to pay their respect to Lula. There was a host of people and the church was full. The service had begun with beautiful songs and there was preaching. Then Jonathan walked up to say good-bye to his wife. She laid there looking so beautiful. He tried to hold back the tears as he read a letter from him to his wife. The letter read "To my dearest love of my life: "I first of all want to say I know that when you passed from this life to be in the arms of God, it was a glorious day!" "So I know that I will miss you, that God has another path for you, and I want you to know that I will love you always and will love your son." "Also, I know that I will see you again!" Jonathan ended his letter by saying "thank you." He got into the funeral car for the very short ride across the way from the church to his family's cemetery. Everyday Jonathan passed Lula's resting place as he went home.

I want to relate to everyone about FAITH, which is God's master plan, and how one decision could have changed the outcome of me not being here.   Everything happens for a reason.   People are placed in your life for a reason.   To my grandfather,   McKinley Newton Senior, "I am just a small part of your legacy and I just want to thank you."

Madelene Yahya